DATE DUE

APR 23 2002			
RCL 2/08			
JUL 2 8 2009			

DEMCO 38-296

SPECIAL MESSAGE TO READERS

This book is published by
THE ULVERSCROFT FOUNDATION
a registered charity in the U.K., No. 264873

The Foundation was established in 1974 to provide funds to help towards research, diagnosis and treatment of eye diseases. Below are a few examples of contributions made by THE ULVERSCROFT FOUNDATION:

A new Children's Assessment Unit
at Moorfield's Hospital, London.

•

Twin operating theatres at the
Western Ophthalmic Hospital, London.

•

The Frederick Thorpe Ulverscroft Chair of
Ophthalmology at the University of Leicester.

•

Eye Laser equipment to various eye hospitals.

If you would like to help further the work of the Foundation by making a donation or leaving a legacy, every contribution, no matter how small, is received with gratitude. Please write for details to:

**THE ULVERSCROFT FOUNDATION,
The Green, Bradgate Road, Anstey,
Leicester LE7 7FU. England
Telephone: (0533)364325**

THE LAST DAY OF SEPTEMBER

Mary Dickinson's husband, Trevor, walked out on her, leaving her with two children and a bitterness which she could not overcome. To pay the bills, she went to work at a local factory, and there she met Calum Fitzgerald. Cal fell in love with Mary and asked her to go and live with him. He didn't know what Mary's marriage had been like, but he had to find out, because as long as Mary hated Trevor she couldn't love anybody else.

*Books by Rosemary Gill
in the Linford Romance Library:*

PROSPECTS OF THE HEART
ONCE UPON A DREAM
GIVE ME TOMORROW

ROSEMARY GILL

THE LAST DAY OF SEPTEMBER

Complete and Unabridged

LINFORD
Leicester

First published in Great Britain in 1992 by
Robert Hale Limited
London

First Linford Edition
published February 1994
by arrangement with
Robert Hale Limited
London

The right of Rosemary Gill to be
identified as the author of this work has
been asserted by her in accordance with the
Copyright, Designs and Patents Act, 1988

Copyright © 1992 by Rosemary Gill
All rights reserved

British Library CIP Data

Gill, Rosemary
　The last day of September.—Large print ed.—
　Linford romance library
　I. Title II. Series
　823.914 [F]

ISBN 0–7089–7512–7

Published by
F. A. Thorpe (Publishing) Ltd.
Anstey, Leicestershire

Set by Words & Graphics Ltd.
Anstey, Leicestershire
Printed and bound in Great Britain by
T. J. Press (Padstow) Ltd., Padstow, Cornwall

This book is printed on acid-free paper

For my mother with love
and thanks for all the Sundays, the
 sunny days,
the shopping days, the special days

1

"WHAT did you say to Fitzgerald?" Susan asked when the silence had gone on for a long time.

"I told him I'd think about it." Mary did not take her gaze from the garden. Susan's garden was not especially pretty; the grass was scrubby from the children playing and almost covered in buttercups. An old wheelbarrow, rusted, stood at the far end. A few straggly yellow poppies flowered beside the fence.

"What is there to think about? You need the money. He did offer you more money?"

"Yes."

"Much more?"

"A lot. At least I consider it a lot. I don't suppose he did."

"So what reservations have you?"

"Oh," Mary turned and smiled at her, "I like the job I have. Mr Patten is nice to work for."

"You mean he's married and fifty."

"Something like that. He's good at his job and we understand each other. I feel as if I'd be letting him down."

"You'd be letting yourself down if you didn't go for a better job and more money."

"I'm not sure I can do it," Mary admitted.

"Cal Fitzgerald obviously thinks you can. Are you frightened of him?"

"No, of course I'm not," Mary said, "he's not frightening. He's not much older than I am."

"Isn't that frightening?"

Mary gave up.

"It is a bit," she said. "Daunting. I can't even afford to dress as the chairman's secretary. What if the children are ill? What about school holidays? Going from part-time working for the personnel officer to full time and the rest for the chairman ... I don't know, Susan, I don't think I can do it."

"Don't you need to do it?"

"What does that mean?"

"Self-respect. He must think you can do it. Once you've made the decision the rest is detail. I can take the children if they're ill and during the holidays. You'll have more money and you will dress to suit. Tell him yes. Go on."

"What if I can't do it? I wasn't made for a career. I was quite happy as I was. If . . ."

Susan went over and hugged her.

"I know," she said, "have a think about it and I'll get you a gin and tonic." She smiled and went off to the kitchen.

Mary got up and walked as far as the patio doors and she wondered what she would have done without her sister since Trevor had walked out and left her with two children. Before things had gone wrong she had been basically a happy person. She had enjoyed being married, enjoyed making interesting meals, looking after the children, doing the gardening, going out dancing. Trevor had announced on her birthday that he had somebody else and he had left the same day.

She looked out across Susan's untidy garden and her eyes filled with tears. The children's song came to mind.

> 'The big ship sails through the alley-alley o,
> The alley-alley o, the alley-alley o,
> The big ship sails through the alley-alley o
> On the last day of September.'

The thirtieth of September. It wasn't just her birthday any longer, it was the worst day of her life.

★ ★ ★

Cal was playing chase with his brother's two children. They were screaming with excitement as they ran round the garden. Even when Annabel told them to stop and offered him a cool drink and shooed them away they were still laughing. She and Cal sat on the patio on high-backed chairs.

"You'd make a very good father."

"Sorry, Annabel, I'm booked for tonight."

She looked disapprovingly at him.

"Are you busy tonight?"

Cal looked warily at her from his dark eyes.

"That depends," he said.

"I'm not trying to get you off with anybody. I gave that up ages ago. We're having a few friends to dinner, that's all. I thought you might like to stay. Kathy and Trevor are coming and Phil and Samantha. It's just casual. You don't even have to go home and change."

"Thanks but I think I'll pass."

"Tom says Trevor's ex-wife is going to be your secretary," Annabel said. "What's she like?"

"She's blonde," Cal said.

"Like blondes, do you?" said Annabel, who was dark.

"Uh-huh."

"Seriously, Cal."

"I don't know. I can't say I care. She's damned good at what she does. Bob should know."

"Isn't he furious with you for pinching her?"

"He hasn't said so."

"He'd hardly say so, would he?" Annabel said, clouting him lightly with the *Independent* magazine. "Trevor's most disparaging about her."

"Trevor's an idiot."

"He's very successful."

"It doesn't have to be a contradiction."

"Don't get clever with me. Come and peel the vegetables."

Cal followed her into the house. The garden was just to his taste; parts of it couldn't be seen from different angles and there were lots of trees and lawns and various shrubs, sloping paths which disappeared into trees, a drive long and edged by tall fir trees. Inside everything was new, the curtains and matching blinds in cream velvet, the carpets blue-grey and cream, but there were toys in the rooms, in summer the house smelled of flowers and there were vases of them everywhere. In the winter it was all log fires and soft lamps. The kitchen was a big square room. Annabel had prepared most of the dinner earlier, fish mousse, lemon sorbet, chicken in mustard sauce, crême brulée. While Cal peeled vegetables she poured gin and tonic.

"Not for me, thanks. I'm driving."

"Oh, get it down you," she said, "I haven't invited another woman to dinner, I swear it to you."

"Bossing you, is she?" his brother observed as he walked in the back door with a bag of golf clubs.

"Did you win?" his wife enquired.

"No. Is that gin for me? Thanks."

"Have mine," Cal said.

"Aren't you staying? Oh, come on. Don't leave me to Trevor's tender mercies."

"Does he know that his ex-wife is about to become the chairman's secretary?" Annabel asked.

"She hasn't agreed yet, Annabel," Cal warned.

"She's a single parent with two children," Annabel said crisply, "that doesn't give her a lot of choice. I hear she's blonde."

"She's a stunner," Bob said.

"Is she?"

"Isn't she, Cal?"

"She's not bad," Cal said.

"My God. Praise, indeed. Have you finished those carrots?"

★ ★ ★

The chocolate factory smelled sweet, Mary thought, as she walked down the corridor towards his office, or was it the smell of success? The factory was only five years old. Most things in the town were new. The 1950s here could have been the Middle Ages. The factories were new, the shopping centres were just built, only the parish church was turn of the century with its high spire and it had been built from commercial gain. The old Odeon cinema had been replaced by a ten-screen complex. There was a better, more polite side to the town, where people like Cal and his friends lived, but most people crowded onto newly built estates like the one where she lived.

Past the other directors' offices Mary walked until she reached the end of the corridor. Through another door and it had no name on it.

It was the bareness of his office which Mary noticed when she was ushered in for the second time in her life. No photographs, no paintings, no books, no plants. There was no drinks cabinet, no sofa, no papers, no easy chairs, just a big desk, telephones, computer, two chairs, one at either side of the desk. He got up. That surprised her too. He was tall, lean, dark and younger than any of the other directors, younger than most of the middle management, and he smiled at her. She was not deceived as she had been at first, thinking that he meant something special by his friendliness. He treated everybody like that, he knew everyone's name.

"Sit down. Tea?"

"No. No, thank you."

They sat down. He looked straight across at her. She remembered that from the first time. Usually men looked her up and down. She was used to it. His eyes were the colour of smoke from autumn bonfires and about as readable.

"So. What did you decide?"

"I didn't. I mean . . . " Mary looked down at her hands. "I need the money. I have two small children and a mortgage but I don't want to start the job and then find that I can't do it. Also I think you need someone to be here more than regular hours and my children are my priority. They have to be. I wouldn't want to make mistakes, let you down."

"Why don't we try for a month and then if it doesn't work we can go back to where we were? How would that be?"

"Is that possible?"

"Of course."

"That sounds fine . . . fine . . . "

"Cal," he prompted.

"Yes? Right. Thank you."

★ ★ ★

Mary looked out over her mother's neat back garden. Everything was in squares, the lawn with its border, the rose garden, the fence. Her mother and father must have been the neatest, cleanest generation in the history of people, she thought. Each day her mother vacuumed and dusted. Every week she turned out all the cupboards and drawers, she washed all the kitchen cupboards. Every year she decorated the house inside. Nothing was thrown away. The tea-set in the china cabinet, sadly out of fashion, was preserved as carefully as if it had been worth money. The house was her mother's god, the garden was her father's.

"That man's divorced," her mother said now from the kitchen sink, her back rigid with disapproval.

"So am I."

"It wasn't your fault," her mother said.

"I'm not going to marry him, Mother, I'm only going to work for him. It'll pay much better than the job I have now."

"Yes, and our Susan'll have to have your bairns while you're at work. She has two of her own."

Mary had learned to say nothing. She paid Susan to look after her children but their mother didn't know that. She couldn't talk to her mother about money or she got an hour of how Trevor had left her, how Trevor should pay her more maintenance, what a dreadful man Trevor had been. Her mother made tea, strong dark brown tea. It was all right if you put sugar in but Mary didn't take sugar and found the brew difficult to swallow.

"You will be careful, won't you, Mary?" her mother said now. "They can say what they like about times changing but men have always tried to take advantage of women and they always will."

When Trevor picked up the children for the weekend in his Range Rover he looked hard at her and said, "Congratulations. I hear you've been promoted."

Mary was about to tell him that it was only a month's trial and then didn't.

She thought of her empty weekend. She would clean the house, walk the dog properly. She missed the children. After he had left they were everything to her. She felt so crushed; the failure of her marriage; the huge responsibility of being the sole adult. There was no one else to take the children to the doctor. She buried the cat in the garden. She took the old dog to the vet to be put down. She would pay the bills and face the dawn and the postman. Some of it was almost funny: the crises rushed her, like runners reaching the tape. Just after Trevor left the electricity failed every day for two weeks. How hard it was to wake in the night and feel for the torch beside the bed, the house silent and so full of darkness. The car tyres went down ten times in ten weeks. The children had influenza and measles one after another and she spent hours huddled on the sofa with them, watching the rain pour down the windows. Philip, who was four, wet the bed every single night. He did it for months afterwards and when things were settled legally and Trevor came to collect the children to stay overnight Philip would run to him shouting gleefully, and on Sunday afternoons would scream in her arms, kicking and fighting as his father's car disappeared around the corner out of sight.

"I hate you!" he would shout at her.

"The chairman's assistant," Trevor said now.

"What?"

"Isn't that what they glorify secretaries to, these days?"

"No, I'm just his secretary."

"You'd have been better off with Tom," Trevor said, "he's a person. His kid brother's a bloody machine."

"I like him."

Trevor grinned.

"Leaping to his defence already? Now that's what I call a secretary," and he went off down her front path, whistling.

★ ★ ★

September had always been Mary's best time until Trevor left her. All the songs about September, the poems and the tunes were part of the cycle of her life. Before then there had never been a bad September. She claimed the fall, the autumn as her own, that time of expectancy, with Christmas far enough away to be exciting without the panic, with the mornings and evenings still warm and light enough to be enjoyed. She loved the early mornings, the stillness, the mist, the sun rising through pale cloud. She loved the fat brambles in the hedgerows, the mushrooms spotted white in the fields. She loved the country in autumn. She tried not to think about the country that September. She concentrated on money.

She went out that Saturday and bought herself a new suit, an expensive suit and a white silk blouse and high-heeled shoes. The suit was blue and black, the shoes were blue. She had her hair cut and blow-waved so that it fell just to her shoulders. The suit brought out the blue of her eyes.

She was early to work. She wanted to get there before him but she was to find that no matter how early she arrived or how late she left he was always there. That didn't stop Cal from saying lightly as she brought in the important post, "You look good."

"Thanks."

He was easy to work for; that was a big surprise. It was also a relief. By Friday Mary was relaxed. She sat in her sister's garden with a gin and tonic and announced, "He's a peach, Susan. I think the man should have been a teacher. He makes everything so simple."

"Teachers don't make any money," Susan said. Her husband taught.

"He's got a mind like a knife blade, so sharp and clean. He makes everything look obvious, even the most difficult things. He doesn't lose his temper, he doesn't snap, he isn't moody."

"You've only been there a week, give him a chance."

The following week Mary went looking at new houses. She had

convinced herself that she couldn't afford to move but she had to get out of there. She wanted to move to where Susan and John lived but it was very expensive, even at the cheap end. She didn't live far from them but her area was quite different, full of people who were failures, people without money, people who had no jobs, no future, no hope. The children were badly dressed and it was very noisy. Often her little boy got into fights and she did not dare to let her children beyond the garden at night. All the houses in the cul de sac except hers had been burgled and the house was so small that she could not even park her car outside.

More and more she thought of the house in the country where she and Trevor had lived but she knew that thinking of the past would not help. Trevor and Kathy lived about a mile beyond Susan and John's house and they had the kind of house which Mary could not bear to think about, large, detached, in its own grounds.

She went looking at the kind of house she could almost afford and hated all of them, they were so poky and in such awful areas.

It was a bad time of year to try to sell her house, Mary knew: the mortgage rate had risen to a higher rate than it had been for seven years — but at least her house was cheap. She walked around her garden, looking at the last of the summer flowers and knew that was all she would miss, not her neighbours, who were scruffy and did not garden. The days were cool now, the golden haze of autumn was settling around the red and yellow leaves. Her garden was big for the size of the house, the fences were high around it. She had paid to have the fences erected. The lawn was neat and her flowerbeds were weeded, even sculpted and she had gardened so that different plants appeared at different times and there was always colour; and not just that, she had flowerbeds all one colour, one white, one blue, one pink. Susan thought that she was slightly dotty but she knew that she was right. It was like having an extra instinct, this knowledge of colour, it was something that changed her world, heightened it, made her feel as though she had some kind of identity, some place. She felt the strength of her independence, even if she was weighed down by responsibilities.

Responsibility was nothing compared to the slow awfulness of her marriage to Trevor.

★ ★ ★

Mary's lifestyle didn't change because of her new job but certain things did. She bought several new things for the house. She had her car serviced, she was able to pay the bills and feed her family. She began to go out occasionally with Susan, just to the cinema and for an Italian meal afterwards but it made a change. The shops in the city were full of Christmas gifts, all dazzling with lights and glitter. Mary hated Christmas, partly because there had been such good Christmases when she was younger, when the children were small, before Trevor had left. Since then Christmas was one continual pile of bills; it was also an empty bed, long nights and no one to buy her anything pretty for Christmas Day. Not that Trevor had been any good at such things, she told herself honestly. He once bought her a washing-machine. How romantic.

November was wet. Trevor came to collect the children one Friday night and arrived early. He had a brand new pale blue Range Rover, which filled almost the entire street outside her house.

"They aren't ready," she said. "You aren't meant to be here until six."

"I want to talk to you," Trevor said.

Mary hated him to say that, it meant that he wanted something.

"What is it?" she said.

"Kathy and I . . . that is, I was wondering whether we could possibly have the children on Christmas Day?"

Mary glared at him and she thought that Trevor looked older. He really did. She was pleased and she thought of Cal; he was the first man who came to mind, working with him every day. How had Trevor turned so ugly, so middle-aged, balding so he had grown a beard? He was out of condition too, he was overweight. Mary thought of Kathy going to bed with Trevor and didn't envy her.

"You have the baby."

"They'd have a wonderful time," Trevor said. "They could play with the baby and if it's mild there's all that garden to play in. We've planned a massive train set for Philip in the attic and a computer for Vicky and lots of other things. Please, Mary, I know they want to come."

"Have you discussed this with them?"

"No, well, I mean . . . I was just so excited."

"What am I supposed to do on Christmas Day?" she demanded and then wished she hadn't said it. Why should Trevor care? He had never cared and she must not look vulnerable.

"Don't you usually go to your mother's?"

Mary conjured a picture of sitting at her mother's, watching films on television, her father asleep by the fire, her mother and her aunt gossiping and knitting.

"They want to come to us, Mary, they're bored at your parents' house on Christmas Day. There's nowhere for them to play and your parents are too old for the noise of two small children. We have plenty of room."

"We had plenty of room too — " Mary began.

"Oh, don't start that again," Trevor said angrily, "if you don't want them to come then forget it. They were the ones who suggested it, not me, if you must know. They want to come. They love the house and the garden and they love the baby too."

I hate Christmas, Mary thought, as she watched him take the children down the garden path. Vicky danced and laughed beside him. Philip climbed happily into the Range Rover. I hate the shadows on the ceiling and the days afterwards all full of nothing. I hate the selfishness of Christmas. I hate the spoiled brats my children have become. I hate the bad news and the accidents, the artificiality and the glitz, the way it never snows and the presents I don't get and the way other people dress up and go to parties.

On the Sunday evening Philip came to her.

"We are going to Dad's for Christmas aren't we?" he asked carefully.

"If you want to," Mary said. That week she found work difficult. Christmas was the busiest time of year in the factory. They not only worked for the season, they made new designs for Easter and new ranges and even more classy chocolates were planned for the following year. When she had joined the company early that year they had already sorted out what they were doing for Christmas and it was not just the chocolates, both traditional and new, it was wrapping and box design, paper, colour, presentation, advertising: image was very important and the company small, with its own shops and a very high-class image. The chocolates were expensive.

They had also had several fights on their hands. Chocolates were fattening, sugar was bad for you. The advertising had to be subtle but Mary knew that even though it was fashionable to be slim it would never cease to be fashionable to give very exclusive chocolates. Orders flooded in and so did the problems. That week it seemed to be worse than ever and on the Friday Mary discovered that she had made a mistake, an important mistake. She had mixed up two companies with whom Cal was trying to do separate deals. He said little to her and Mary thought that she was not upset. She kept telling herself that she wasn't, that it was almost the end of the afternoon. She went back to her office and worked for an hour and then without any warning she burst into tears. She was about to escape to the ladies' but Cal chose that moment to walk into the office. She turned away.

"I'm sorry," she said.

"I said it was all right."

"It isn't."

"It will be. I'll sort it out."

Mary sniffed, choked, the tears ran. Cal put down the papers in his hand and got down beside her. Mary couldn't believe that either, Cal down at knee level, close, closer than any man had been for years, Cal in his expensive suit. Whatever would anybody think if they came in?

"People will think I've yelled at you," he objected. "It's only chocolate. It puts holes in your teeth. Why don't you go home, it's nearly four o'clock. See your children."

"Trevor's taking them to karate."

"So . . . let's get the hell out of here."

2

THEY drove. They left Mary's old car and they left the cold autumn afternoon. They drove into the darkness. Mary didn't care where they were going, she didn't think he knew. Driving like that was so comfortable; she rather hoped that the journey would not end. The radio sauntered out nondescript melodies, the city lights were gone, only car lights now, people going home. She thought of people going home to one another. She could remember what it had been like, Trevor coming home to her, the evening brightened, interrupted, the weight of the children being shared. They used to have dinner when the children had gone to bed, he used to talk to her, laugh with her, make love to her. She looked across at Cal, driving.

"Where are we going?"

"I don't know. Where would you like to go?"

"How about the coast?"

"Right."

It was late afternoon when they arrived. Rain was falling into the dark sea. The hotel was white and floodlit and rain fell down past the orange street lights and all around the black trees. They stood for a little while and listened to the big sea roaring and let the wind sweep rain across their faces, and then they walked up the steps into the hotel and sat by the fire in the big lounge. Mary felt like a pampered child.

There was tea and hot muffins with glistening pots of strawberry jam, sandwiches cut like diamonds, salmon and cucumber, cakes very unsubtly oozing cream, a silver teapot steaming, and china cups so thin you could see your fingers through them.

"Is that better now?" Cal asked.

"Yes, thanks."

"It's been a heavy week."
"Yes."
Cal looked hard at her.
"So don't tell me," he said.
"It's Trevor. I feel like I want to go all the way up the street and put my fist through every window I come to. I get so angry."
"Are you angry with him?"
"God, yes, I could kill him, or stand outside and scream and scream."
They stood outside. Mary didn't scream. She walked up the wet beach and then she ran down it and she watched the lighthouse, far off on its tiny island. The rain stopped and they walked back to the car and then they got in and drove again, further up the coast. The night cleared, the moon graced a silver sky, they reached the city.
"Do you want a drink?"
Mary said that she did and they went to his house. She was surprised. She had imagined either that he lived in a huge house in its own grounds or that

he had a modern sleek flat. The house was terraced, in a reasonably polite area but nothing flash, a small square lawn in front, a long narrow hall inside with a door in the porch which had stained glass. There were plaster faces carved where the hallway arched.

The floor was chequered black and white. The house was warm. The stairs had a spindled staircase. She followed him through into the kitchen at the back. Mary thought it was the most comfortable kitchen she had ever seen. Again, the windows had stained glass around the edge and there was a big cream Aga. He found a bottle of burgundy and two glasses, since Mary had expressed a preference for red wine, and they went into what her mother would have called the front room, a biggish room with a large bay window. The chairs were comfortable rather than new and there were several shelves of books and a television. The fire was the nearest thing to real, it was gas with flame.

"This isn't at all how I imagined you lived."

"How did you think of it?"

"Rather like Trevor and Kathy, a big house, grounds or a smart flat. Did you live here when you were married?"

"No. We couldn't afford anything like this. We had a nasty little terraced house. It's a long time since. I was eighteen."

"That's very young."

"That's why it didn't work, I think. I thought I was going to be the biggest thing since Terence Conran. Only I wasn't. I made a mess of things and she went back to her mother."

"What did your parents think of it?"

"Not much. Especially since Tom worked respectably and married respectably."

"But you're very successful now."

"I'm also a lot more careful. I can't believe you were married to Trevor."

"Oh," she sat down in the chair across the fire. "Trevor wasn't always a complete nit. When he had hair on his head and not on his chin he was sometimes quite desirable. I think his brains fell out with his hair."

He said nothing for so long that Mary looked up.

"You hate him," Cal said.

"Yes. Isn't that awful?"

"What did he do to upset you so much this week?"

"He wants the children on Christmas Day. I know it doesn't sound like a big deal but it is. He has Kathy. They have.. they have a child. They have a great big house . . . "

"Don't you have anybody?"

"Yes, my mother and father and my sister."

"I meant — "

"No." Mary spoke quickly and took a swift gulp of wine. "I don't want that again. I couldn't ever put myself into a vulnerable position like that. I want different things now. I want a nice house, a nice car, pretty clothes. To be able to go home and close the door and for nobody to ever — for nobody ever . . . the children want to be there, a lovely big house with big gardens. They love it. He bribes them. He buys them toys and . . . I hate Christmas."

"Do you have to let them go to him?"

"No, but they want to. What do you do at Christmas?"

"Sleep."

"Do you?"

"Yes. Last Christmas I lay in bed all day."

"That's terrible," Mary said, laughing.

"No, it isn't. It was nice."

"But you have a family."

"The idea of watching Tom's kids opening their presents and going to church with my parents didn't appeal."

"But you could have gone somewhere if you'd wanted to."

"I could have but I was tired."

Mary nodded.

"You work too much," she said.

"I like to. I get a kick out of it."

"Even today?"

"Will you stop worrying about it? It was nothing. The world will still go forward. It is the only mistake you've made. Do you like the job?"

Mary tried to hide the smile but couldn't.

"I'm amusing to work for?" Cal asked.

"Better than that."

"So far."

"So far."

★ ★ ★

The new sales director took a shine to Mary; that was what the other girls said. The new sales director was young, single, drove a white Porsche, had a car telephone and wore expensive grey suits which set off his golden hair and white smile. Michael Addison turned up in Mary's office when Cal wasn't around.

"I'm busy," Mary protested after he had wasted fifteen minutes of her time.

"Have lunch with me."

"Haven't time."

"Oh, come on. I'll take you somewhere nice."

"Cal wants this report this afternoon. Now please."

Michael slid off her desk, holding up both hands in defence.

"I'll go."

He went just before Cal walked into the office.

"What did Addison want?" he asked.

"Lunch."

"Did he now?"

Mary worked through lunch, had an egg sandwich, finished the report. The following afternoon Michael walked into her office again.

"Are you going to the Christmas party?" he said.

"I don't know."

The party at Tom and Annabel's was an annual event and since it was being held on Christmas Eve this year and she was going to be alone Mary had thought she might go. She had also seen a dress she wanted which she could not afford, silver-skirted with a black velvet bodice and silver jacket.

"I'd like you to."

Mary looked at him.

"You're wasting your time," she said gently. "I'm divorced with two children. Now will you please go away?"

"Mary, you have the best legs that ever walked into this factory, not to mention the rest of you. I like you, and I want you to go to the Christmas party with me."

"That's very kind of you, Michael, but no."

"Why not?"

"Because I don't want to get involved with anybody." Mary slammed shut the filing cabinet and turned around and he was in the way. It was almost comical. "Excuse me."

He moved and Mary went back to her desk and sat down.

"Don't you like me? Hm? Not even just a little?" his voice was soft and wheedling.

"Of course I like you."

Michael lifted his eyes and then he glanced at Cal's office door.

"The boss?" he said.

"What?"

Michael nodded towards the door.

"There has to be a good reason."

"I told you the reason," Mary said, losing patience. "Now will you please go? I have a lot of work to do."

After he had gone, after he had shut the outer door with an irritated click, she was shaking. Cal was away from the office all day. Mary worked very hard.

★ ★ ★

Christmas was worse than ever this year, it seemed to go on and on. She thought that the shops were decorated earlier, that the television advertising started sooner and that the dresses were prettier than they had been. She didn't want to face Christmas without the children. It had taken her weeks to tell her mother and after her mother had been angry all she said was, "You can come to us."

"No, I . . . " Mary hadn't known that she was going to refuse. "I've been asked to friends at work and I . . . they've been kind to me."

She embroidered on the friends so that her mother would not be offended but her mother was relieved, she could see. The children talked constantly about Christmas Day. Mary went out and bought herself the expensive dress with the black velvet bodice for the party and then she spent a full day worrying about it, wishing that she didn't have to go, hoping that somebody would say 'why don't you come with us', thinking that the children might go down with 'flu. The party was on Christmas Eve, that was what really decided her. The children would have gone to Trevor's by then and she knew that if she had to stay by herself on Christmas Eve and Christmas Day it would be unbearable. She was so miserable that Christmas Eve. She had wanted the children back on Boxing Day but it was clear that they didn't want to come.

When they had gone, when Trevor had come in his brand new Range Rover and collected them, she shut the front door and stood behind it and put her hands over her face to stop the tears and then she went calmly upstairs to get ready for the party. She deliberately made herself late and then couldn't face the idea of not being able to drink so she telephoned for a taxi. The night was frosty. The taxi dropped her off just outside the house. She saw gratefully that Cal's Mercedes was there but when she walked in the first people she saw were Trevor and Kathy. That was a shock. She could also see Sam and Phil Thompson and a number of other couples whom Tom and Annabel were friendly with. She smiled towards various people she knew but they didn't see her. Nobody greeted her. They were all in couples.

Nobody tried to draw her into the various groups. Mary backed out to the hall, thinking that she might go and nobody would notice. She backed into somebody and turned quickly. It was Cal.

"Trevor and Kathy are here," she said and walked past him outside. The night was starry. Cal followed her out, she heard his shoes crunch on the ice.

"Come in with me," he suggested.

"No, I can't. I don't want them to think . . . " She began to walk down the drive and then stopped, remembering that she didn't have a car.

"I'll take you home," Cal said.

"No."

"It's a helluva long walk."

"I don't want you there. I mean . . . I don't want you to see the place."

"You think I'm made out of chocolate, don't you?" Cal said lightly.

She smiled at him but she said, "The

area's very tacky."

Cal didn't appear to be listening closely. He put his hands on her arms and when she divined his intention she started to move away, began to say no and then she stopped and looked up at him and when he kissed her she put one hand up to the back of his neck and drew him nearer. It was not that she wanted him to kiss her, it was just that she didn't want him to stop. He was so warm and so tall, he blotted out the night, he blotted out the party, the hurt, the way that Kathy and Trevor had wanted the children so that she was alone but had left them with a babysitter to go to a party. She got herself closer to him so that he stopped kissing her and pulled her against him and she put both arms around his neck and closed her eyes even tighter. When she let go Cal walked her to his car.

The dog ran to greet her, didn't even bark at Cal. The house was quiet but the area around was never quiet. People were partying and the noise came through the walls. Now in the dim hall she was remembering Trevor's lovemaking, not how they had been together and in love at the beginning but how it had been before he left, negligent, unspontaneous; and from somewhere the anger outweighed all the other feelings, and when Cal turned her to him it wasn't hunger she felt, it was an overwhelming need to get rid of Trevor. She thought that if he didn't understand, if there was anything tentative or hesitant about him she would run away. But Cal wasn't a young man in love, he wasn't out of love either, she realized. He wasn't bored, he wasn't careful and he was big enough to be lost against. She shut her eyes and leaned in at his shoulder for ever so long and the noise from outside and the narrow hall with its cheap shaky staircase didn't matter. Then she put on the lights and led him upstairs and into her bedroom where the pillows sat high in the middle at the top of the bed. She switched on the pale green bedside lamps. She took off the silver jacket and went back to Cal to have him kiss her bare throat and neck and shoulders and pull down the thin straps on to her arms. The dress, she thought, had already been worth the money. She started to undo the buttons on Cal's shirt and then she looked into his eyes and suddenly she was happy, laughing, putting her arms around his neck, her fingers into his hair and he held her in his arms close, pressed against him, and then in the soft quiet of the night he slid down the zip at the back of her dress and put his hands on to her soft skin.

★ ★ ★

In the night they had bacon sandwiches and a bottle of pink champagne which she had been saving for Christmas Day.

Mary didn't recognize herself, naked in bed, drinking champagne with a man she didn't know very well, a man she worked for, a man who was not in love with her, whom she was not in love with. It was against everything she had imagined she stood for. Casual sex, she told herself later, but there was nothing casual about it at the time. Cal was young, enthusiastic, imaginative and had the kind of confidence that money and success gave people. In the night Mary was someone quite different from herself, no pretence, no hanging back, no restraint.

It was quite different than she had ever been with Trevor; Trevor had not worn expensive clothes, a Rolex watch. Cal didn't have inhibitions. He wasn't older than she was, trying to prove anything. He was rich and successful and it showed in bed. Mary laughed to herself. Maybe that was why women liked men who were rich and successful, not because they could provide an illusion of security. Cal Fitzgerald didn't give a damn about her, he was enjoying himself. He only cared whether she was having a good time now. Trevor had liked to hold her down and have her and have control. Cal was nothing like that. He didn't go for control. Mary thought that was strange when he did so with, as far as she knew, every other aspect of his life. He gave her confidence. She thought that was funny too because in a way he did just the same thing at work. He didn't try to make her feel inferior, he was so easy to be with. Before the night was over she felt like she had just been to the best party of her life, she was tired and satisfied and happy, warm in his arms.

She awoke in the middle of the morning with the feel of the duvet against her skin, not quite sure where she was. She opened her eyes, thinking it had to be a dream and there he was, the man who paid the wages.

Oh no. I didn't, she thought and pulled a pillow over her head. Did it have to be him? Why couldn't it have been Michael Addison? She took the pillow off her head and looked at him.

Forget Michael Addison, she thought. If you must have a one-night stand this man was perfect, saving the fact that he was her boss. Mary groaned inwardly. How could I have been so stupid? she thought. She slid out of bed and found a nightdress, pretty, white, clinging stuff, and she stood by the window. The morning was dark, the day was raining and thick fog. She closed her eyes and sighed.

"I can always sing 'Who's Sorry Now'," he said softly.

Mary turned and looked at him.

"How about 'It had to be you', or rather 'Why did it have to be you'? Only I know the answer. You're the only man I know that I like, trust and fancy like hell. But I shouldn't have done it."

"Why ever not?"

"I don't want to get involved with anybody."

"Who's involved?"

"You mean it?"

"I mean it. Come back here and stop

worrying about things."

Mary went back and sat down on the bed beside him.

"I have to work with you."

"Not until a week on Wednesday you don't," Cal said, putting one hand on her neck and kissing her mouth.

★ ★ ★

Later she put on a dressing-gown and went down to let the dog into the back garden. She made some tea and took a tray back to bed. When they had drunk the tea Cal presented her with a small square package.

"What's this?"

"It's a Christmas present, idiot."

"But I didn't buy you one."

"I'm meant to do the buying, remember?"

"I've only been there three months."

They were earrings; diamonds, with long drops like tears.

"Good God," Mary said, "after three months. What do I get next year, a

Mercedes? Oh Cal, how beautiful, how impossible! I can't take them, especially now."

"Why especially now?"

And Mary hesitated for the first time. This wasn't Trevor, whom she knew, or Michael Addison, whom she knew was simple.

"After seducing you."

Cal laughed.

★ ★ ★

The day cleared. The sun came out, it was warm. They drove to the seaside and walked the dog along the beach. There was no one else on the sand. They parked the car up on the sand dunes and walked to the ruined castle. It was meant to be closed, the National Trust notice said so, but nobody was about so they climbed over the gate and walked up. The castle was set high, the rocks were sharp and steep, sea-spray soaked the first rocks, the tide was in. Mary looked out over the water on one side and over fields on two. She looked back to the tiny village and she felt again that surge of happiness and the feeling that followed was one of suspicion. They walked back to the car, Cal threw sticks for the dog and they had hot soup and ham sandwiches. It was the strangest Christmas lunch that Mary had ever eaten.

The sun was so warm they sat outside on a bench and watched the gulls on the sea wall and the boats moored in the harbour. As evening drew in they drove back to town and Mary made a pot of tea. She saw Cal looking around her tiny dining-room cum sitting-room.

"Awful, isn't it?"

"It's a bit grim, yes, but you've made it pretty."

"You should have seen the place we had before. More than anything in the world I'd like a nice house. That's why the children like to go to Trevor and Kathy's. They have a gorgeous house."

"Why don't you forget about Trevor, he's a fool."

"He's rich, successful, like you."

"I'm nothing like Trevor."

"No, he's not as clever as you are, nor half as rich, I imagine."

"Why did you marry him, he's years older than you?"

"I was very impressed with him. I thought he had brains."

"What impresses you now?"

"Nothing. Only diamonds," and Mary shook her head a little so that the earrings glittered and sparkled. Cal leaned over and kissed her just under her right ear. "Are you going now?" she asked him.

"That's up to you."

"Don't tell me you haven't been invited anywhere. I don't believe it."

"Well, we can go to a party if you like, or to supper at my brother's but I'd much rather stay here, or if you like we can go to my place. There's smoked salmon and fillet steak and red wine."

"Can Rex come too?"

They ate by candlelight with a pretty pink cloth on the table and crystal glasses and then they sat on the sofa by the fire and drank brandy.

"Your house is very comfortable," she said. "Trevor and I had a beautiful house in the country. He took it all."

"How did he do that?"

"He just did, he's cleverer than I am and my solicitor was a man. I think he considered it fair. He got the money, I got the children and the dog. Now he isn't even satisfied with that. Trevor would be happy if I was out on the street."

"But you're not. You have a good job, a wonderful boss, a better salary. Why don't you move?"

"I'm going to."

"I'll help you to find a house."

"Will you?" she hugged him. "I love my job. I didn't before. It was just necessity. It's very exciting. No, it is," she said, as Cal began to laugh. "You find it exciting too. You like the people buying what you make."

"It pays the bills," Cal said.

"Oh, come on. You like being the best."

"What else is there to be?" Cal said.

3

MARY thought that being in the office with Cal would be more difficult now but it wasn't. He left on Boxing Day because the children came back in the evening and she had the children the weekend of the new year. The children went back to school and she went back to work. Work was as hectic as ever. Valentine's Day was the next important occasion and they were working for Easter. There was also Mother's Day to be kept in mind and a big new chain store had ordered supplies of expensive chocolate permanently for its shelves. Mary thanked God for sentiment and 'sweet tooths' and worked hard.

The first weekend of the New Year she was planning to see Cal. Trevor wasn't taking the children until the Saturday morning. Mary was going to

Cal's house in the evening. He was due back from Germany that day.

Trevor took the children and then he telephoned. Mary was surprised.

"Is something the matter?" she asked.

"No, nothing. I just want to talk to you without the children. Can you meet me at lunchtime?" He named a small cheap café in the centre of town.

Exactly at half-past twelve Mary walked into the little café thinking that if this was nothing important she would stay in town for a little while afterwards and do some shopping, but the sick feeling inside made her suspect that afterwards she wouldn't want to do any shopping. Trevor was sitting at a table by the window. He was smiling. That, Mary thought, was a bad sign. Trevor was only pleasant to her when he wanted something. He ordered a lavish meal. Mary had a small sandwich and a cup of coffee.

"Is something wrong?" she asked.

"No," Trevor said. He spoke softly. Mary's stomach began to churn. "It's something important and I don't know how to talk to you about it." He hesitated. Mary's appetite left her and, since her sandwich arrived then, she gave it a sickened glance and ignored it. Trevor attacked his mince and dumplings, pausing between forkfuls to say, "Kathy and I have been thinking about this for some time. It isn't something we've jumped into. I mean it isn't a sudden decision, because it's very important and I know it's something Philip and Vicky want: I talked to the children at the weekend but I asked them not to say anything to you until I'd spoken to you."

Mary said nothing. She wanted to cry. She wanted to run. This was like a re-enactment of the day that he had left her, his apparent concern, his gentle tone. She sat there wishing that he would not sound so reasonable, wishing that she could curl up into a ball and roll away. She thought of how quiet the children had been since the weekend, how they talked in whispers together. Trevor finished his mince and dumplings, scraping the last of it up from the plate with his knife, bricklaying it neatly on to his fork and into his mouth. Then he put down his knife and fork and looked at her.

"The thing is that Kathy and I love them very much and we'd like to give them a home." Like they were orphans, Mary thought later. "We want them to come and live with us. If you saw the children together you'd understand." He spoke quickly as though it was well rehearsed. "They all get on so well. We have a lovely big house and they want to come and live with us."

"We had all that," Mary said, almost strangled, "and you spoiled it. They only want to come to you because you give in to them all the time, over-indulge them, you give them everything they want."

"We can afford it."

"Because you don't pay me sufficient maintenance."

"Kathy and I can give the children a better life," Trevor said patiently. "It's them we're thinking about, not us. It'll be a lot harder with four children — "

"Four?"

"Kathy's pregnant," Trevor said sheepishly. "It'll be a lot harder in all kinds of ways but we have to think of them and so must you."

The waitress had stopped at the next table with two plates of beef curry and rice. Mary reached out and slipped her hand under one of the plates just as the waitress put it down. She picked it up and tipped it over his head. Then she ran out of the restaurant.

★ ★ ★

Snow fell during the afternoon. Mary lay on her bed in the warm room and watched it fall. The telephone had rung several times since she got home and she had not the list to answer it. She didn't remember how she had driven home. Snow had been starting to fall then and she had been so shivery, like she was starting with 'flu only she wasn't. She lay there until the day was so dark that she could see but only just, because she had no lights on. The she heard the doorbell. She didn't get up. The noise went on and on like somebody was leaning on it. When she decided that it was not going to stop she walked slowly downstairs, clutching the banister rail. Rex was barking frantically.

She threw back the bolts. Cal stood there. He was wearing a black coat, covered in snowflakes.

"Whatever's the matter?" he said. "Are you ill? I knew you were there and I've tried telephoning and . . ."

Mary looked at him and smiled and then her hands shook and her legs wobbled and she couldn't. Not only could she not look up but without any warning at all she started to cry, not gently or discreetly but the kind of wracking sobs with which she had cried herself to sleep night after night when Trevor had walked out. During all that time there had been no one to comfort her. Cal swore softly and then he got her inside and sat her down on the sofa and put both arms around her and Mary turned in against his shoulder. She did nothing but cry against him for a long time and from there with his arms fastened around her she was able to say, "Trevor's trying to take the children."

"He can't do that."

Mary sniffed and sat up.

"He wants the children to go and live with him and they want to go. I knew they did, I knew at Christmas. They're so happy when they're with him." She smoothed a hand across the front of Cal's shirt.

"I got it from London," he said.

"What?"

"My shirt."

Mary gave a wobbly smile.

"You're very patient."

"I'm very clever too. Don't worry, I'll help you."

Mary shook her head.

"I thought things couldn't get any worse. I mean ... I thought they were getting better, my job, you ... I mean ... Cal ... You do wear nice clothes."

"Don't I?"

"Trevor can't wear clothes with any style. He's too fat."

She looked up into Cal's calm dark eyes. "I tipped curry over him in this cafe in town. He's bribed the children with his money and his lifestyle. They like the big house and the gardens, the toys and the new clothes. I suppose you can't blame them for that. Trevor and Kathy, they ... they have everything. I thought he was happy. After all, he and Kathy have a baby with another on the way. The children are everything I've got."

"You could fight him."

"I know but what point is there, what

pleasure when they don't want to live with me? God knows I don't want to live here myself and I'm never here for them. They're always at Susan's and ..."

"You were talking about moving."

"It's not just that."

"What?"

"Children all want two parents and the kind of ... they want to go back to what we had before. It won't be the same obviously but it's a lot nearer than anything I can give them. It isn't just the material things, they remember how we were before and you may not believe it but in the beginning it was good. I mean ... I think they remember it as being good."

"But it wasn't?"

"I don't know now. I'm looking back with Trevor having left me. I don't see it properly. It was fine, at least I thought so then. It wasn't until afterwards I saw how it had been. I'll never go through that again, giving in to what Trevor wanted, making what

Trevor wanted to eat, watching what Trevor wanted on television, pandering to his moods and keeping the children quiet because Daddy was tired. He was so important. How did men ever get to be so important?"

Mary stopped. Dear God, she thought, a speech. Where did that come from? She released herself from Cal and he shifted back, stayed quiet for a few moments and then he said, "So what do we have?"

"What do you mean?"

"Let's consider the possibilities. It's a lifestyle you need if you're to get what you want. You have to get the children to want to be with you. Provide what they need. Either that or change your life totally, let them live with Trevor and Kathy."

"I don't want to think about it any more just now," Mary said, cuddling in against him. "I can't think any more."

★ ★ ★

The following afternoon Cal telephoned.

"I've got an idea," he said. "Are you interested?"

It was a cold bright winter afternoon. He drove her to the smart side of town. There in the most luxurious part he stopped the car at a huge set of gates. He turned the car in at the circular drive. There was a white Toyota parked outside the stone house. Mary climbed out of the car. The house was old, the chimneys were high and stone and the windows had lovely stone mullions. The gardens were overgrown so that the gardener in her was longing to explore. Cal introduced her to the estate agent who got out of the Toyota. Mary thought that he had lost his wits but she allowed herself to be walked around the house.

It was the kind of house that she thought nobody would ever want to leave. It was empty of furniture, the low sun shone through the stained-glass windows in the hall. The kitchen was long and wide and had its own garden just outside the back door. All the rooms had pretty, old-fashioned fireplaces. The drawing-room was huge, the dining-room a big square room opposite the kitchen. Upstairs were two bathroom and six bedrooms, all big with views of the white countryside. From there she could see fields, horses, trees and the sun shining on the river. The gardens looked even more exciting from upstairs and when she and Cal strolled outside after the estate agent had gone, she had to stop herself going off to look even more closely. Paths led away into the distance. Willows touched the ground.

"What do you think of it?" Cal asked.

"I don't know. If I understood what was going on I might be able to tell you."

Cal paused for a moment and then he said,

"What if we were to buy it?"

"What?"

"You and me."

Mary looked hard at him to see if he was making jokes. Cal didn't say anything. He stared down across the lawns.

"I ought to buy a bigger house and I've always liked this one. It would solve your problem."

"It would create a lot more, I can bring at least a dozen to mind now. I think you've been designing chocolates too long. This isn't 'once upon a time', you know. It's mad."

"No, it isn't. We could have it all drawn up legally. It would be OK and when one of us wanted out we could sell."

"Nothing would induce me to do anything of the kind," Mary said flatly.

"Even to keep the children?"

She turned away, the garden suddenly looked cold and dark, the light was going from the day, the long winter evening beginning to draw in. She hated it all so much now, hated the short days, the long nights, the seasons, everything.

"I promised myself that I would never again do such a thing and I won't," Mary said and she walked away from him across the wet lawn to the tall trees at the far side of the garden. Cal followed her.

"Will you please stop being angry and use your brains? Do you know that Trevor could re-apply for custody and possibly win? He's married, he has a very good income, a house in a nice area, a stable relationship. You don't have any of that. And the courts look carefully at what the children want. They want to be with him."

"Stop it, please. You're making me say things I shouldn't. You shouldn't have brought me here. I couldn't do it. I couldn't be under an obligation like that. I put up with running about after you at work because you pay me for it and that's all. Now I want to go home." She turned around and tried to move and Cal got hold of her.

"Do you like the job?" he said.

Mary looked bitterly at him.

"Is it like that?"

"Mary, I'm not Trevor, don't hate me. I'm not trying to blackmail you. I mean that I hope you like your job a lot because it could be all you're left with. That's all I'm left with and it isn't much fun."

"I can't shout at you, Cal, let go of me."

"Shout at me. For Christ's sake shout at somebody. Do you want the children or don't you? How much do you want them?"

"I won't go back to that."

"Nobody's asking you to go back to anything. I thought you were a fighter. You fought Trevor for custody, didn't you? You got yourself a job and a decent house — "

"I won't live with a man. I don't care for you and you don't care for me. A few nights don't make a relationship, Cal, and even if it did that's not what I want. You know that. I want independence. I want a house and a car and new clothes and I will get them for myself. I won't wait around for men to — to buy diamonds for me. Going to bed with you is very nice. It makes me stop thinking about Trevor but that's all. What I really want from you is a job."

"You've already got that."

"Then let go of me. I don't want to put that in jeopardy." They walked back to the car in silence. "There is one thing you could do."

"What's that?" Cal said, without looking at her.

"You could try not mentioning it for a few days. It might make things a bit easier."

★ ★ ★

Mary could not resist driving past Trevor's house that evening. The winter night was dark. She even stopped and sat in her car for a few minutes. Then she turned the car around. As she went past the house again they were just getting out of their blue Range

Rover. The children were dressed in expensive casual clothes. The house was brightly lit. She thought that she could see firelight. Trevor opened the door and they went inside. She tried to visualize her life without the children but couldn't.

She crept into work on the Monday morning. Cal behaved as if nothing had happened, as if they were nothing to each other. He did this so successfully that Mary could hardly stand it. She couldn't sleep, she couldn't eat. By Wednesday afternoon she found courage to ask for some holiday. Cal didn't even look up.

"We're busy," he said.

"I need some time."

"Forget it. A couple of days won't solve the problem."

"Some sleep might."

"You won't sleep, you'll worry and if you're here at work at least you haven't time for that."

"I need to think," Mary said, putting her hands on the front of the desk.

"You have thought. You're avoiding making a decision about it. You think that the problem will go away. Well it won't. Either you find a lifestyle so that you can keep the children or you let Trevor and Kathy have them. You can go on doing nothing about it and Trevor and Kathy will get them. Then you lose."

"I don't like the alternatives."

"It isn't a question of whether you like them. It's a question of how much less you dislike them than losing the children. Have you anybody else you could buy a house with? Another woman with a child? A relative? No? How about Susan and her husband? Your parents?" Mary was shaking her head to all these. "There is another possibility. We could live in the house separately. We don't have to sleep together. You're not the only woman in the world."

"And what are you getting out of it?"

"What I was getting out of it

originally, a bigger house, a better market — "

"A housekeeper?"

"No. I already have somebody to cook and clean."

"Money then?"

"When we sell it, it should do well if the housing market goes up and it does, sometimes with a hiccup or two."

"I know that," Mary said slowly. "Thank you very much for the offer but I can't."

Cal bunched some papers together and got up.

"Don't I have a board meeting about now? Fine," and he walked out of the office.

It was only then that Mary realized she was afraid. She was effectively going to give up the children because she was afraid that Cal would treat her as Trevor had. She thought of her life without the children and she was suddenly very cold. She ran out of the office after Cal. The corridor was empty.

4

MARY didn't look at Susan. She couldn't.

"How ever did you get yourself into such a mess?" her sister sounded weak with amazement.

Mary didn't answer. The garden looked better under snow, smooth and tidy as it never was. Even the wheelbarrow looked picturesque.

"You went to bed with him? I thought you couldn't stand men. I thought you never wanted to live with one again."

"I don't."

"Nice in bed, is he?"

"Yes."

"You idiot, Mary."

"It's all right you saying that," Mary said, trembling. "It's all right for you. It was Christmas Eve and I was . . . I was damned miserable."

Susan got up from her shabby brown sofa and put both arms around her sister.

"I do understand but did it have to be Cal?"

"No," Mary moved away, "it didn't have to be. There's a perfectly gorgeous sales director who drives a white Porsche and is tall and blond."

"And you didn't want him?"

"Not a bit. Not even a fraction. I didn't mean to go to bed with Cal but . . ."

"Does he think you're in love with him?"

"No."

"Is he in love with you?"

"Not in the least."

"But you liked going to bed with him. Mary — "

"I know but sometimes and just sometimes the idea of going to bed with somebody as thoroughly delectable as Cal is just too much to withstand. It's like promising yourself you'll never drink champagne again or buy yourself a nice dress. You can mean it first thing in the morning or when you get your bank statement but after a little while . . . And I went to that party on Christmas Eve and the first people I saw were Trevor and Kathy. I went outside and Cal was there and he kissed me and . . . I didn't want Trevor to have been the only man in my life, that's all. Cal gave me diamonds for Christmas. What am I supposed to do, turn into a saint?"

Susan looked hard at her and then she said,

"Well, I'm sorry to tell you this, Mary, but the man has got to be in love with you. What other reason does he have to house a divorced woman with two small children and a dog? He's not a saint either you know. And if you go and live with him you can hardly deny him your bed. And what happens when it doesn't work? You may have been ready for a one-night stand but you certainly aren't ready for another relationship. What are you going to do about working together when you prove this to him?"

"I wish I knew."

"You know that you don't have any alternative, don't you?"

Mary nodded. "But that's not exactly fair to Cal."

"He's not a moron. He knows life isn't fair. So go and tell him yes and hurry up before he regains his sanity and changes his mind."

★ ★ ★

February was wet and miserable. Tom Fitzgerald drove home through several miles of slush into the arms of his wife and a swift Scotch. He was late. The children were in bed and the dinner was only microwave fresh.

"You look tired," she said, kissing him.

"It's been a long day. I'm beginning to wish that Easter had never been invented."

"Oh, darling, all those chocolate

bunnies," Annabel said laughing.

They sat down together and then Tom eyed her.

"Got some news," he said.

"Good news?"

Tom took a mouthful of lamb casserole and shook his head.

"My brother is buying a house with his secretary."

"Heavens. Do your parents know?"

"No."

"She's very pretty," Annabel said.

"She's divorced with two children. Can you imagine what my mother will say? A divorced blonde. I think he's in love. He must be to do anything this stupid. She must be after his money, Annabel."

"Why must she? Cal's a dish. He's gorgeous."

"Thanks."

"You're married and gorgeous."

"From what I hear her ex-husband is trying to take the children. I think he's out of his mind."

"I expect you've told him so."

"Have I hell. The last time I told him to do something he was ten and I was thirteen and I was bigger than he was. Who's going to tell Mother?"

"Well, I'm not."

★ ★ ★

The children liked him. They had been cautious for the first few seconds but Cal turned out to be that most rare of men, he liked children. Mary thought he wasn't even aware that he did so. He gave them his time, he would play games with them for hours, he liked rough physical games or Monopoly or just sitting in front of the television. It was a quality Mary had not expected to see. She got quite a shock. Cal was eight years younger than Trevor — was that the difference? — but Trevor hadn't gone on like this. Perhaps it was making sweets, Mary thought, perhaps Cal was so successful because he wasn't really an adult. He sat on the floor in her living-room and played board games with them for hours. When they went to look around the house he ran about the lawn with them and Victoria shrieked and screamed and laughed while he caught her and flung her up into the air and caught her again. Inside, the children ran upstairs, choosing a bedroom each. Mary stood silent, watching the winter sun play through the stained-glass windows in the hall.

She had not even told the children what was happening. Childlike, they had assumed they were part of what was going on, were welcome. They did not question whether they were going to live with Trevor until the end of that day when Philip came cautiously to her and said, "Are you going to marry Cal?"

"No," Mary said, putting the last of the dishes away.

"But he's going to live with us."

"We're going to live with him."

"Are you in love with him?"

Philip was watching too much

television, Mary decided.

"No."

"Then why is he going to live with us?"

"Because he offered and because I hate living here."

"So do I. Vicky and I think the new house is the best place in the world. We even like it better than Daddy and Kathy's."

And that made it worthwhile.

★ ★ ★

Trevor and Kathy soon heard, Mary didn't know how, but the following Saturday, which was not Trevor's weekend for having the children, Trevor's car pulled up beside her house well before nine o'clock. He rang the doorbell and when Mary answered he walked in, something he had never done before, in spite of Mary's pale pink carpet and his dirty shoes.

"I want to know what the hell's going on. There's some story going around that I just don't believe about you and Cal Fitzgerald buying Grey House."

"We are, yes. Isn't it an awful name?" and Mary tightened the belt on her dressing-gown and returned to the kitchen. "Tea, Trevor?" she asked as he went after her.

"You and Cal Fitzgerald? What is this, an office romance?"

"No, it isn't," Mary said evenly.

"What is it then?"

"It's an arrangement."

"What sort of arrangement?"

Mary sipped her tea from where she sat at the small table and couldn't help but think rather happily of how the new year might be, the new house, the new garden, the next spring, the following September.

"What sort of an arrangement?" Trevor said again.

"I don't think that's any of your business."

"You did this on purpose to stop me from having the children. I didn't think you'd do such a thing, you devious little cow. Getting somebody like Fitzgerald to lay you for that. You're not right. He'll be bored with you in a month and he'll put you out. You're like a bag of potatoes in the sack, Mary, you always were. No imagination. Going to bed with you was one of the biggest disappointments of my life. It was like opening a present all nicely wrapped with ribbon and glossy paper and finding there's nothing inside."

Mary thought of how Trevor had been in bed. Had she hated being there with him or were her memories coloured by what had happened since? After the early days Trevor didn't bother with anything but the act itself. She knew women who boasted about how long their husbands could go on making love to them, she remembered some woman at work moaning about how lousy her husband was in bed. 'Just a few seconds and then — bang!' She remembered lying under Trevor and waiting and waiting with her eyes shut and her face averted and Trevor doing his sexual press-ups. It didn't vary much, it just went on and on like a kind of nightmare. And then she thought of Cal but it was strange, she thought, strange how she had made love to Cal in a way that she never had with Trevor because there was no commitment, no bills, no marriage certificate, no pressures. She thought of Cal laughing and his gentle voice and the way that he had encouraged her. It was just play to Cal, it was not duty. It was casual, fun, pleasure. Cal would never make a husband, he didn't think like one. He didn't threaten, or feel threatened, he didn't moan, he didn't care. That was right for now, she thought, somebody who didn't care.

She and Cal went looking at furniture that day. Mary was cautious at first, most of the money involved wasn't hers but he went on as if there were holes in his pockets. They bought the kind of furniture which Mary had always wanted. She started to think that she was in some kind of dream. Cal was happy with expensive Chinese rugs, they bought a pink and blue one, very big, to go over the polished wooden floor in the drawing-room. He insisted that they bought a sofa big enough to lie on and leather chairs for the study and an Edwardian oak desk which Mary fell in love with. The dining-room was oak too, the chairs had pale mushroom leather seats, the table was marked like honeycomb. They looked at Wedgwood china and Waterford crystal glasses. Mary was dazzled, guilty.

Late in the day, tired and happy, they visited Marks and Spencer for convenience foods. They watched television. The children went to bed; Cal fell asleep for a few minutes just after ten o'clock. Mary watched him sleep and when he opened his eyes he smiled and she hadn't known until then that she was staring.

"What?" he asked softly.

"Nothing, I just . . . I was wondering what it would be like living with you."

"I've been living with me for years. It's pretty good."

"You may get tired of the children."

"Very probably."

"What will you do then?"

"They go to bed."

"Sometimes."

"I'll only be tired of them sometimes. Don't you get tired of them?"

"Yes, but I'm related."

"Not being related is good too."

"You may get tired of me."

Cal looked at her while Mary waited for the answer.

"It isn't going to be like that," he said. "This isn't marriage, it's called outwitting the opposition. I'm very good at that but I wasn't much good at marriage and I have no intention of setting myself up to be shot down again. I want my own room and my own space and it cuts equally." Mary deliberately said nothing. "You haven't got past Trevor yet. You hate him too much to allow any room for anybody else."

Mary frowned. "I managed before Trevor left."

"And you had a wonderful marriage until then."

"It was dreadful. Trevor came over this morning. He's furious about the house and us moving in together. He was awful with me. He told me I was like a sack of potatoes in bed."

Cal smiled a little. "And what was he like?"

"Awful."

Cal sat up. "It sounds to me like a real case of incompatibility."

"It's called marriage," she said. "You said your marriage was dreadful."

"It wasn't dreadful. I was young and broke and she didn't like being broke. She went back to her mother."

"I'll bet she's sorry now."

"I don't think she is. She married happily and had two children. They're not terribly well off but he takes her dancing on Saturday nights and they spend the weekends as a family. If you can manage that what else do you need?"

★ ★ ★

Mary's father and mother disapproved and said so. She tried to explain to them that she was only doing this because of the children and her mother looked sideways at her.

"You tell me that you haven't been in his bed, our Mary, and I'll believe you." Mary couldn't stop the colour that rose in her cheeks. "I thought so," her mother said. "I've seen the lad — "

"It's nothing to do with that. He doesn't care about me." Mary realized the minute the words were out that they were wrong.

"No, you can bank on it. He doesn't need a woman with two children. He can have any little bimbo he wants — "

"Mother!"

"He's rich. Rich so he doesn't have to care, and good-lookin' an' all. You'll never hold him."

"I don't want to hold him," Mary said, stung. "He provided a way out, that's all. Even if it doesn't last I have to try it. I won't let Trevor have the children."

"You think you're clever," her mother said, plonking down the iron with force, "but I don't want you hurt again. That Trevor, your father and I could have killed him for what he did to you, and now look. Calum Fitzgerald. My God, our Mary. And whatever will his parents think? A lad like that from a good family."

"Mother, he's nearly thirty. He's not a child. He's not going to listen to them."

Her father got up at this point and walked out of the kitchen and banged the door.

"I wish it was the spring," her mother observed, "he's no good without his garden."

★ ★ ★

Tom was in Cal's office, looking out of the window at the unexciting scene below, the factory yard, the vans, the roads, windows.

"I had Father on the telephone last night. He'd left half a dozen messages on your Ansaphone."

"Oh yes?"

"They found out about Mary. Why didn't you tell them?"

"There's nothing to tell."

"You buy a new house, you're going to move in with your secretary and her two children and there's nothing to tell them?"

"It isn't like that. It's just a convenient and financial arrangement, that's all."

Tom looked cynically at him. "Tell me this. Did you or did you not kiss the girl in my garden on Christmas Eve?" Cal looked up, about to object. "I saw you, Cal. You didn't come near us for two days afterwards. Now I'm not a curious man but when you decide to move in with her I come to obvious conclusions."

Cal said nothing.

"Well?" his brother prompted.

"You always were fairly obvious," Cal said and only grinned when Tom swiped him round the ear.

★ ★ ★

They moved into Grey House at the beginning of spring. Mary had had no difficulty in selling her little house. Cal's house took rather longer to get rid of so that she panicked slightly, wondering whether it would work out.

She found her joy hard to contain. The house was carpeted and curtained to her taste and satisfaction. She spent a lot of her free time in the garden watching happily as the spring flowers began to appear, first snowdrops and then crocuses, followed by daffodils. Each day there were new things to see and in the house comfort and the smell of new furniture. A cleaner came in. Mary tried to keep the place tidy and it was easier than a small house. Being used to living on his own, Cal was tidy. He could also manage, unlike Trevor, to load the washing machine when necessary. The cleaner did the ironing. Mary organized the children as she had always done.

Cal, like many people without children, didn't eat breakfast and was in the habit of lying in bed until the last possible minute before going to work. Mary had instructed the children that they were not to go to his room, especially early in the morning, or into his bathroom, so that Cal might have some privacy — but he was too much of a novelty for that.

The house was exactly right. The children were sometimes reluctant now to go to Trevor and Kathy's. Mary took great pleasure in driving them there in Cal's white Mercedes. Cal was a good babysitter but Mary had nowhere to go. Her sister's husband had given up teaching, had found work in Libya and since she couldn't find a babysitter the small social life that Mary had petered out. She discovered that she didn't mind. Staying in with Cal was quite different from staying in alone even if they didn't crowd each other.

The children ate when they came home from school; Mrs Briggs fed them. She was a good cook and there was always something like a casserole to re-heat with salad, so Mary and Cal ate at half-past seven at first and after the first few days they took to putting the children to bed and eating afterwards. It was, to Mary, like having a small comfortable dinner party every night. She didn't have to cook, there was a dishwasher, Cal liked to have wine with dinner and they talked about work. It was more fascinating than Mary would have admitted even to herself. He told her all the important company secrets that other people didn't know. She loved the involvement, she found it exciting. She liked his ideas, pored over the problems. When he was away, which he quite often was, she missed having dinner with him.

Cal seemed determined not to crowd her. Sometimes he went out. If he didn't he often left her in the drawing-room. He would lie on the sofa in the den and drink beer and watch sport on television and it wasn't long before Mary got tired of sitting in splendour on her own. If the television was on it was the only light in the den.

The room had a thick carpet and a very big sofa; they could both lounge on the sofa in comfort. Cal would make space for her, sit with his arm around her. Affection was something Mary had not experienced before. Often she fell asleep against him there. She liked the darkness, the flickering light of the television and Cal's comfortable silence. Sometimes they listened to music. She would sit back and close her eyes and listen and not worry about anything.

Annabel rang and invited them to dinner.

"You said 'yes'?" Cal asked, wide-eyed.

"Shouldn't I have?"

"Does that mean you want to go?"

"I thought we might."

"Your ex-husband and his wife will probably be there."

"I don't know."

In a way it was satisfying to Mary to be asked. She went out and bought herself a simple expensive dress in a soft blue material. It suited her better than anything she could remember buying. She was astonished when she came down the stairs on the evening of the dinner party and Cal was lying on the sofa in the den wearing a shirt and a pair of jeans.

"Aren't you going to change?"

He didn't take his gaze from the television.

"I am changed."

Mary thought for a moment.

"Won't the others be wearing suits?"

"Probably."

"We'll be late," she said.

When they got there she quelled the desire to walk in as though she had some kind of physical claim on Cal, he looked so good. The first person she saw was Samantha Thompson, blonde hair shining, green eyes glittering. Her dress was green like a sheath and very expensive. Annabel kissed him on the mouth but Mary thought that Samantha Thompson might just as well have done. All through dinner Phil Thompson's wife made soft conversation with Cal. She was sitting opposite. Mary was astonished and not very pleased with herself at the way she felt. Jealousy hit her like a shovel. Annabel and Tom made bright conversation. Neither Samantha nor Kathy spoke to her and Trevor didn't even look at her. Phil Thompson talked to Trevor about business all night. In the car on the way back she said nothing.

"You're very quiet. Didn't you like

the dinner party?"

"Annabel's very nice."

"Yes, she is."

When the babysitter had gone Mary stood in front of the fire. Cal poured brandy for himself. She had refused some.

"Can I ask you something?"

"What?"

"Are you sleeping with Samantha Thompson?"

Cal stopped pouring brandy for a second or two.

"Whatever made you think that?"

Mary's eyes filled with tears and as he turned to her she looked down. "Kathy and Trevor used to look at each other like that and then he left me."

"I'm not sleeping with her," he said.

Mary raised her eyes, blinking. "It's awful for the other person," she said. "You can't imagine how awful it is."

"I said I'm not."

"Then you already have done," Mary said.

"It's none of your business," Cal said tightly.

"She's married — "

"I said it's — " Cal made himself stop. "You don't understand."

"Oh yes I do. Kathy was prettier than me. She had no children to hold her down. She had time to dress and put on make-up. She wasn't fat round the waist because she'd just had a baby, sloppy with milk and tired from getting up every night with the children. She had time to talk to him and listen. She had energy to go to bed with him."

"Phil was already sleeping with his secretary."

"How predictable," Mary said.

"Oh, I don't know." Cal considered his brandy. "I slept with mine."

Mary didn't move, she didn't even stop looking at him until a tear spilled over and then she tried to get out of the room and Cal swore and put down his brandy and got hold of her.

"I'm sorry. I didn't mean to say anything half as awful as that."

Mary closed her eyes and shook her head and the tears ran and she pulled free. Upstairs in her room she wished there was a lock on the door but she stopped Cal in the doorway when he followed her.

"Don't you come in here. Don't you ever."

"Mary — "

"Don't you justify yourself to me. I don't want to hear it. Shut the door."

When he had gone she cried herself to sleep.

5

CAL was missing most of the next day. He came back in time to say goodnight to the children and then he went off to the den. Mary went to bed. Monday was more difficult. They drove to work together. Nobody spoke. At the end of the day Mary put a typed sheet on to his desk.

"What's this?"

"It's my notice."

Cal picked up the paper and then he looked up at her.

"That's not fair."

"How fair were you?"

Cal got to his feet.

"I didn't do anything," he said.

"Yes, you did. You slept with Samantha Thompson and then you slept with me."

"I didn't."

"Yes, you did. I was there, remember, and you said on Saturday night that you went to bed with her."

"I don't mean I didn't. I mean I ... oh God, I don't know what I mean any more." He looked at her. "You want me to have, don't you?"

"Why should I want that?"

"OK. I went to bed with her. It was very nice too. Will you take back the notice?" He handed her the piece of paper. Mary took it and walked out of the office.

From then it all changed. Cal no longer came home to dinner. Sometimes he didn't come back at all. He wasn't there for the children, who complained bitterly that he didn't play games with them. He wasn't available for social events. They were two people living in the same house, just as she had intended they should be. Cal almost lived at the office and when he was at home he stayed in the study and worked.

At first Mary thought that she didn't

care. She tried to pretend that he didn't exist except at work. The problem was that Cal had been so easy to live with. They had laughed a lot. At first it was a relief to find that Cal was just like Trevor, that he was as bad as everybody else. She told herself that men were all alike. She spent days ignoring Cal but it was hard to ignore somebody who was the boss at work and then didn't bother to come home. Also she saw him at work, making the decisions, taking the knocks, living with the things that went wrong. She knew the way that his shoulders went down when he was tired. And then one warm early summer night she couldn't sleep and she ventured downstairs and the light was on in the study. She opened the door softly and he was asleep over the desk. Mary got down beside him and stroked his hair.

"Cal. Cal, darling, you can't sleep there. Come on."

"Leave me alone," Cal said without opening his eyes.

"You ought to go to bed."

"No."

"Cal," she said loudly and he opened his eyes and looked at her.

"What time is it?"

"Three o'clock."

"Is it?"

"How long have you been asleep?"

"About half an hour," Cal said, sitting up.

"Would you like a drink?"

"No, thanks."

He began tidying the desk. Mary watched him.

"I'm taking the children to the fair tomorrow. Will you come?"

"I've got a meeting."

"It's Saturday, Cal."

"I know what day it is."

"I'm going out tomorrow night. Shall I get a babysitter?"

"No, I'll be here."

She hadn't been out for weeks and Susan's husband, Peter, was home and had promised to look after the children. Susan knew that something was wrong but Mary hadn't told her. They were planning to go and see a new film but the queue was so long when they got there that they couldn't get in so they went to a pub nearby which did a good bar meal. They ate. It was crowded later but that didn't stop Michael Addison from pushing his way through to see her.

"Well hello," he said. "Can I buy you a drink?" Mary said no at first but he persuaded them and when he went off to the bar Susan said, "Who's that?"

"It's Michael Addison. Don't you remember me talking about him?"

"Is he single?"

"Very."

They had two drinks. It got late and Susan wanted to go back. He insisted on driving them back, though they had planned to get a taxi. The lights were on in the kitchen when he dropped Mary at the back door. He even leaned over and kissed her. Cal had just boiled the kettle.

"Would you like some coffee?" he asked as she walked in.

"Yes please. Did the children go to bed all right?"

"Yes. I took them out for pizza. Did I recognize the car there?"

"It was Mike. We met him in the pub. He talks about work all the time. I think Susan was bored."

"Weren't you?"

"I like talking about work."

Cal handed her a cup of coffee and Mary went off to the den and put her feet up on the sofa. The nights were still cool and a log fire burned low. Cal followed her in and sat down.

"He asked me to have dinner with him on Monday. I'll have to get a babysitter. You're away all week, aren't you?"

"Until Sunday."

Cal left early on the Monday morning. Michael Addison took her to the most exclusive hotel in the area. He was well-mannered, well-dressed, polite, courteous, attentive. He talked freely, he listened, he didn't drink too much, he drove her back, kissed her on the cheek and went home. On the Wednesday they went to the cinema, on Friday he took her drinking. On the Sunday evening she invited him inside and he kissed her on the sofa in the den. Mary put her arms around his neck. Michael looked at her.

"What am I getting here, full marks for trying hard?"

"What?"

"Mary, my love, you're pretending I'm the boss."

"I am not. I wouldn't do such a thing. He's — "

"Due home?"

"I wouldn't do that. He's not due for hours yet. I told you this is just an arrangement."

"You told me a lot of things," Michael said. "I tried hard to believe them because I really would like to go to bed with you but I'm wasting my time."

"I didn't think that was what this

was about. I don't want to go to bed with anybody."

"Don't you?"

She heard the car, heard the back door.

"I thought you said — "

"It was right."

Mary hurried through into the kitchen. His bags were on the floor and Cal was unknotting his tie.

"You're early," she said.

"I couldn't wait to get back," Cal said flatly "took an early flight. Hello, Michael."

"How did it go?"

"They went for it."

"They did? At our price?"

"Yes."

"That's great."

"Have you eaten?" Mary said.

"All I need is some Scotch."

"I must admit I wasn't sure you'd pull it off," Michael said. "Does Tom know?"

"I rang him."

"That's wonderful."

Mary handed Cal a glass of whisky with ice. He took it gratefully and thanked her. Michael left. When she came back from seeing him out Cal was still standing with his back against the work surface.

"Are you sure you don't want something to eat?"

"No, thanks. How are the children? Did Vicky go to the dentist all right?"

"Yes. She wasn't very keen but I let her put her tooth under her pillow. Unfortunately the tooth fairy forgot to take the tooth. I'd been out and had rather a lot of wine . . . that was Friday. And Phil got a hundred per cent in his intelligence test. Trevor was pleased about that — "

"What did you do with the Scotch?"

"I put it away. Did you want some more?"

"Yes, please."

"Come and sit down. I lit the fire in the den."

Cal took off his jacket and sat on the sofa with her. Two coffee cups stood on the little table there. Only one small lamp was lit.

"Did you go somewhere nice?"

"We went out for dinner. We went to Smithsons the other night; just for a pub meal tonight. We went to the cinema on Wednesday."

"Nearly every night then?" Cal said, putting down his glass.

"Just about."

Cal looked at her and then he said.

"How about something you haven't done with Michael this week?"

"Like what?"

"Oh, I don't know. That sort of depends," and he got hold of her with both hands.

"Cal . . ."

"Just answer me this then. Why?"

"He's . . ." Mary moved back and he let her. "He's harmless."

"Harmless? You mean he's not Trevor."

"Something like that."

"I'm not Trevor."

"No, but you're not harmless either."

Cal didn't have time to reply. The telephone rang just behind him. He didn't say much at first, for a longer time than she could remember anyone not saying much on a telephone. Cal was so alert now. She sat there, waiting while he said terse things like "Are you certain?" "Do the papers know?" "OK. Yes, thanks."

When he finally put down the receiver Mary switched on the lamp nearer to them.

"What's happened?" she said.

Cal looked at her like it was the middle of a bad dream.

"It was the police," he said. "There are two people in hospital, an MP and a television personality. They were poisoned by our chocolates." He got up and walked out of the room. Mary followed him down into the kitchen where he put on his jacket and picked up his car keys.

"Where are you going?"

"Tom's. Ring him for me, will you?"

"How were they poisoned? How do

they know it was our chocolates?"

"They think it was. That'll be sufficient for the press."

"Couldn't it have been something else?"

"It could. Just keep your fingers crossed."

★ ★ ★

Mary sat alone in her office, the early summer sun glinting in through the window. Cal was in a board meeting which had gone on all day. It had been confirmed that the chocolates were to blame. Irish terrorists had claimed responsibility but no one had said how many more chocolates had been poisoned.

Susan took Mary's children. She thought Cal might like some peace when they drove home in the middle of the evening. Outside the factory crowds of journalists waited and when they got home he had difficulty in driving the car though the gates for another crowd.

When they walked in the telephone was ringing. Mary immediately unplugged the telephones, put a match to the drawing-room fire, took a big squat glass from the cupboard, flung half a dozen ice-cubes into it and filled it with Scotch. She handed it to Cal, who was sitting on the sofa in the drawing-room, quite still.

"Are you going to bed?" she asked him.

Cal gave her a swift look but said nothing.

"You haven't slept in two days."

"I don't want to sleep, I just want to be temporarily deaf."

"The doors are locked, the telephones are out of action, the children are at Susan's and there's food in the refrigerator."

"Yes, but how much Scotch is there?"

"A case of Bell's. I got it this morning."

"I hope I don't need it all."

"So do I," and Mary went back

to the kitchen and uncorked a bottle of Jacob's Creek Shiraz and watched happily as the big glass filled with red wine. She went back to the drawing-room and sat down beside him. She took him into her arms. Cal closed his eyes.

"The chocolates are all going to have to come back to the factory." He pulled ineffectually at the knot in his tie.

"Come here. I'll do it. Can you stand that financially?"

"I have to. If it turns out they were isolated cases it may be all right."

"I don't understand why they chose you."

"I don't know. Because the chocolates are good quality, the kind of thing people like to send. Maybe they think I'm a traitor."

"You aren't Irish."

"My grandparents were."

"It isn't your fault your grandparents left. Your mother came from Surrey, didn't she?" It sounded so comforting.

"You bought a whole case of Bell's?"

"Yes."

"Will you marry me while I'm still solvent?"

* * *

Tom looked back from the lake towards his parents' house. He had so many memories here, mostly of holidays since he and Cal had been sent to boarding-school at seven. He had enjoyed school. Cal had hated it. Cal had fought with other boys, with older boys, argued with teachers. Tom felt an intense irritation as he watched his father casting the fly yet again into the lake. It was early evening.

"You can come and work for me," his father said.

"You're as bad as he is," Tom said. "He takes after you, do you know that?"

"Nothing of the sort," his father said evenly.

It was a perfect evening, warm, cloudless; there were lots of flies about.

A good evening for fishing.

"Calum takes after your mother's side, thank God."

"He's a damned good businessman."

"Oh brilliant," his father said. "He's been down the sink once, he's about to go down again for however many cool millions it takes. He's divorced, childless and living with a divorced woman who has two of somebody else's children. Your brother has made a wonderful success of his life."

"Dad, we're going to need capital."

"Well don't look at me. You're not getting mine. Go to the bank."

"They won't play ball."

"I don't blame them."

"It wasn't Cal's fault," Tom said tightly.

"My money is all tied up. I couldn't get if for you even if I wanted to."

Tom walked slowly back up from the lake and across the gravel to the house. From the kitchen came the smell of cooking. His mother was lifting a roast of lamb out of the oven. She prodded it with a sharp knife.

"What did he say?"

"He said 'no'."

"I told you he wouldn't help."

"But why not?"

His mother looked quizzically at him. "Your father doesn't like you working for Cal. There was no use in him sending you here."

"He didn't send me."

"Your father wants you to work with him. He always did."

"Cal is a raging success. What's wrong with that?"

"You mean he was."

"She's a very nice girl, Mother."

"Hardly a girl, with two children. And likes men with money. She may have come unstuck this time. Everybody is talking about it, all our friends. She's a little nobody, Tom. He needn't think he can bring her here. We know a lot about her, even though Cal didn't deign to tell us. Her parents live in a council house in Edgewood and she was married to that dreadful man who sells gardening equipment and gnomes."

Tom drove home with a noisy rock cassette turned up full blast in the car. His children were in bed but his wife was waiting in the kitchen and to his grateful surprise she had supper ready.

"I'm late and you're an angel," he said but when she put the food on to the table in front of him Tom swallowed two glasses of wine and not much else.

"Your father wouldn't help," Annabel guessed.

"Cal told me not to go. It wasn't that. I expected that. I didn't expect them to be so disparaging about Cal and about Mary."

"That's inevitable."

"Is it?"

"My mother was horrified and I'm not involved."

"I think he's in love with her."

"I think he is too. Do you think Mary loves him?"

"We're about to find out. Maybe she is too."

They were three days into the problem of the poisoned chocolate. It was almost as bad to Mary as the thirtieth of September had been except that this time Cal was there. Neither of the two men had died but both were very ill and the terrorists had threatened that more chocolate was poisoned. Cal had recalled every box. He wasn't sleeping and he wasn't eating.

It seemed to Mary that she couldn't turn on the television without publicity or move without reporters, policemen or unhelpful curious people. It went on day after day until it was normal. She didn't like being without the children but she wanted to keep the publicity from them. Trevor and Kathy were almost smug. They were delighted to have them. She saw a gleam of hope in Trevor's eyes. If Cal went bankrupt it was likely that they would get the children.

All that week she did what she could and Cal worked. The newspapers talked of new deliberate action by the same group which had nothing to do with chocolate. No new cases were reported. On the Friday evening of that week Mary put a plate of steak and salad in front of Cal. He looked at it.

"Cal . . . " Mary pulled out a chair from the kitchen table and sat down beside him, "Cal, look at me. If you don't eat you're going to be ill. Those people didn't die. It will be all right."

"The damage is done," he said, "the orders are cancelled. There's no work."

"There will be."

"Mary, nearly all the capital I have is in the business. I've built and built it and taken nothing from it. It's all I have. You can only have a squeeze situation for so long and then you get to the point where you can't pay your overheads or your workers because there's nothing coming in and it doesn't take long. The value of the business is very little right now, less all the time."

Mary took a deep breath. "Yes, well. Those people could have died. They didn't. Nobody else is ill, nothing else has gone wrong. You're going to make new chocolate and it's going to the shops. The publicity will fade. It will be all right."

Cal smiled at her. "I wonder how many times you've said that to me this week? I almost believe it. I've spent the last seven years building that business."

"Dear, dear, and you so old. Please, Cal, eat it. Not eating isn't going to help. It isn't going to make any difference. It's getting cold."

She left him there just in time to pick up the telephone receiver in the den. It was Annabel.

"Come and have supper with us tomorrow," she said.

"Oh Annabel, that's nice but Cal isn't eating anything."

"It doesn't matter. Come anyway."

They went. It was such bliss to have a meal made, to be asked to stay the night so that they could drink wine and it was a perfect evening so that after supper, when Annabel's children were in bed, they could sit in the garden and heard the faint rustle of leaves in the warm breeze.

"The children are coming home tomorrow night," Mary told Annabel as they walked to the far side of the garden in among the lime trees.

"You must have missed them dreadfully."

"I have but there was nothing else to do. Things have changed so much. I mean ... Cal and I, we weren't ... Annabel, will you tell me something?" She looked up earnestly.

"If I can. What's it about?"

"Samantha Thompson. That night we came here for dinner. I could tell by the way that she looked at him ... We had this dreadful row about it. I don't want her near him but she's so beautiful and ... " She stopped because Annabel laughed.

"I'm sorry but she doesn't hold a candle to you. I do know a bit about it. Tom can never keep a secret from me. I never do from him. Sam was on the brink of leaving Phil. She found out he'd been having an affair — "

"With his secretary."

"Yes. It had been going on for months. I think after Sam had the baby she went through post-baby blues and Phil went somewhere else for comfort. She's very attractive and one night when they were here Phil made an excuse that he had problems at the nightclub he owns and Sam knew that he was going to meet her. He asked Cal to take Sam home. Very bright, I must say. It didn't last long. He broke it off with her when Phil began to suspect something was happening and left his secretary, and I think Sam's pregnant again, but of course when she saw you . . . "

Mary said nothing for several moments and then admitted, "I only went to live with him because of the children. I mean we'd been to bed together but . . . I don't know whether I'm in love or not, Annabel. I don't know how far I'm motivated by money and security and the children. I can't help that. We don't have any friends and he hasn't even introduced me to his parents. I felt like an intruder."

"I wouldn't worry about his parents. They don't like anybody. They don't even like Cal very much."

Mary stared at her. "Why?"

"I think his mother didn't intend to have another child. They thought Tom was perfect. He is of course," Annabel laughed a little, "and I don't think Cal was a very easy child. He hasn't done a single thing they wanted him to do. He left school at sixteen, he married at eighteen and failed in business at twenty and got divorced, and since then there has been a long succession of women and making money and spending it. His parents are very intolerant people but even if they hadn't been I think they might have lost patience by now. As to you having no friends, most of his friends envy him you — "

"Me? but why should they? I have no education, no background. I couldn't hang on to Trevor. I've got two children, no money — "

"You're so beautiful."

Mary choked. "You can't live on that, Annabel."

Annabel hugged her. "You're also very nice. And if your friends don't envy you Cal, they want their heads looking at. You have Tom and me always."

Annabel had put them in the same room. When they went to bed Mary looked hard at the big double bed. "You needn't worry," Cal said flatly. "I never put a hand on any woman who didn't want me", and he went into the bathroom and slammed the door.

6

THINGS changed. The children came home. The publicity died. They went back to working normally. She even hoped that things would be normal but they weren't. Nobody wanted the chocolate, even when the new chocolate had been produced. Cal began to put money into the business, what capital he had, what he could borrow. She didn't dare talk to him about it, about whether it was a good idea. Nobody telephoned except Tom and Annabel. Nobody called and Cal was silent as he had never been. Sometimes he ate and every night he lay in the den by the pale light of the television. He lay there for hours in the evenings. Finally Mary couldn't stand it any more. She waited until the children were in bed one night and then she walked in and said, "I want to talk to you."

"I'm talked out."

Mary switched off the television, switched on a lamp. Cal looked witheringly at her.

"I want to know what's happening."

"You do know what's happening. We're going bankrupt."

"Then why are you sinking money into it?"

"To stop it. Why else?"

"And will it?"

"I don't know."

"You must believe that it will."

"There isn't a great deal else I can do."

"And when you have no more money and can't borrow any more, what are you going to do?"

Cal said nothing.

"You could sell the house."

"It's just a drop in the ocean," he said.

"Sometimes another drop makes all the difference. How much is it worth?"

"I don't know."

Mary sat down beside him, knees under her.

"If you want to sell the house go ahead and do it."

Cal didn't reply.

"Cal, we're not married and they're not your children."

"And that's your opinion, that I would sell the bloody roof over our heads?"

"It's only a house. If you go bankrupt we'll lose the house, our jobs and our financial credibility. I don't want to be poor again. I've been there twice and it's boring."

"If I sold the house you'd go through all that with Trevor again."

"Not necessarily. We could buy a cheap house, it doesn't have to be wonderful, as long as it has three bedrooms and a back garden."

She went into the kitchen to make some coffee. She put the kettle on and then she stood and cried.

"I'll get the house valued tomorrow," she said when Cal walked in.

"I'm sorry."

Mary sniffed and then she turned around.

"I've been very happy here with you and it wasn't the house."

Cal went to her and kissed her lightly on the mouth.

They had the house valued at just under four hundred thousand. On the Thursday of that week Trevor made an appointment to see Cal. Mary was consumed with curiosity and had to wait all weekend before the Tuesday appointment. Trevor breezed into the office. He was wearing a rather loud but expensive suit in orangey browns which Mary took an instant dislike to, and he was in excellent spirits. Nothing cheered people, Mary thought, like the downfall of those they disliked. She kept a polite smile on her face and ushered him into Cal's office. He was in there for quite a while. After he left Cal offered to take her out for lunch, something he didn't normally do. It worried Mary. Cal wasn't eating dinner, never mind lunch. He took her to the Albert Hotel.

"Are you ever going to tell me what Trevor wanted?" she demanded when the order had been taken.

"He offered me a job," Cal said.

"He did what?"

"Managing one of his stores."

"My God," Mary said, "the unmitigated nerve of him. Was that all he wanted, just to score? He spent a long time with you for something that silly." She was looking straight at Cal. "There's something else, isn't there?"

"He made me an offer for the house."

Mary felt like she'd been knocked over, it was so physical.

"He wants our house?"

"He offered me four hundred and fifty thousand for it. Cash."

Mary stared at him across the white tablecloth.

"But they have a nice house. They have a — a better house than he and I had. Much better. Bigger. It's a lovely house. It ... " she thought of the pretty house in the country where she had lived with Trevor, the blossom on the plum trees, the wind in the garden. Her throat hurt with not crying. "Why did you bring me here to tell me this? You said he could have it, didn't you?"

"No, I didn't. I said we would think about it, talk about it."

"What is there to talk about? It isn't worth as much as that." She paused but Cal said nothing. "Is it?"

"No, it isn't." When he looked straight at her Mary got up from the table and ran out of the room. When Cal caught up with her she was standing beside the car, looking out over the back of the hotel, the houses.

"Why would he do that? Why? It's because of the children. If you go bankrupt I'll lose my job and the house and Trevor will get the children because then I won't have a job or anywhere to live. I hate him. I hate him, I hate him."

"Mary . . . whatever happens, you won't lose the children. I'll still be here and you'll get another job and so will I. We'll get another house."

"I don't want Trevor to have our house. You can't sell it to him. Don't you understand what he did to me?"

"Mary — "

"Leave me alone. Take me home." She said nothing all the way back to the house. When they drove around the corner the sun was shining on the windows, the garden was a mass of flowers. Mary ran into the house and up the stairs into her bedroom. Cal went after her. She didn't look at him.

"If you sell our house to Trevor I shall go away and not come back. Maybe that's the point. Maybe that's what you want now that things aren't so rosy. You want to get rid of me. When you're going bankrupt the last thing you want is a woman who has two of somebody else's children. Right, I'll go now," and she got up from the bed and went to the big wardrobe and pulled suitcases out of it.

"Mary, stop it. I haven't told him he could have the house."

"But you will. How could you do anything else, a cash offer of more than it's worth? Are you going to turn that down?"

"You told me the other day that it was just a house."

"Not when Trevor wants it," Mary said, flinging things into the case. "He knows the children love being here. That's why he wants it, and all you care about is the money."

Cal looked levelly at her. "It isn't worth four hundred and fifty on the open market. It wouldn't make that much, times are difficult, interest rates and mortgage rates are high. It might take us months to sell it for a lot less than that. If Trevor wants to score why can't you just let him? All you had from him was grief."

Mary shook her head. "Only a man would see it like that. Trevor likes me being poor, he likes my distress — "

"OK, so he likes it. You like him being middle-aged, fat, bald and lousy in bed. You hate men. You only wanted me for what I could give the children and because I had money. When I went down the first time Eileen left me and you're doing the bloody same thing."

"It isn't true. I — "

"Of course it's true. I don't know what the hell you thought I was getting out of it. Somebody else's lousy kids and a flea-bitten dog. We're going to sell the house to Trevor because he's stupid enough to let his feelings get the better of his bank balance. We aren't going to do that. We'll buy another house — "

"Don't talk about 'we'," Mary spat, "I haven't agreed to anything. I'm leaving."

"If you want to go on hating Trevor that's your problem. I do know what he did, I know what it feels like. Eileen was carrying my baby when she left me. She got rid of it and then wrote and told me so I know. But it's no good going around hating people. It eats away at you. You have your own life and if you can't find any joy in it then it's your own fault. You're living in the past, that's what you're doing, that's why you can't love anybody else. You're obsessed with your hate for Trevor."

"What a lovely speech," Mary said. "You should've been a politician."

"I have to get back. I have an appointment at two."

"Goodness me yes, get your priorities right. That's all you care about, isn't it, your business. Your bloody chocolate factory," and she hit him. She didn't care any more, he was Trevor taking the house from her, Trevor spoiling her life. She couldn't have done anything because of Trevor. She didn't look, she didn't stop to think, she hit him as hard as she could straight across the face and then he did something which Trevor had never done, which Trevor never would have done. He just stood there. Mary waited for him to hit her. She waited and waited. She drew back as far as she could, made herself as small as she could manage and the afternoon sun turned the room golden and he wasn't Trevor.

★ ★ ★

Mary walked slowly down the stairs and out into the garden. Cal was lying on the lawn under the trees. She went over and dropped down beside him but he didn't look at her.

"Please don't be angry, Cal. I'm sorry."

"It's easy to be sorry afterwards."

"I — I thought you were going to hit me."

Cal looked at her then. It made Mary want to run away.

"I haven't hit a woman since I was in nursery school. What gave you the impression I was going to do it now?"

"You shouted."

"So? I don't hit people and I expect them not to hit me but just get this. If you ever do it again the rules will not apply. Understand?"

"Got it," she said flatly.

★ ★ ★

Mary already knew that she could bear anything in her life but Saturday was not easy. Kathy and Trevor went around the house with shining eyes of greed. Mary tried to be pleasant and even went as far as to offer them tea. The sun shone through the trees in at the windows. Mary felt sick with rage and disappointment and envy. The baby screamed almost all the time they were there. Vicky and Philip played in the garden. At least, Mary thought, the children won't lose the house, only Cal and me and I don't think he cares very much. She watched him being polite to Kathy, making conversation with Trevor. He didn't look sad.

What he did look was elegant as

Trevor couldn't look, the fine dark hair shiny, the smoky eyes cool. He looked as though he didn't know what poor meant. His face and hands were tanned from being in the garden. There was a fineness about them. Mary glanced at Trevor and he frowned at her.

The children were going back with them. She watched the Range Rover cannon down the drive and she thought how ugly it looked. It would have looked right on the moors with dogs and rugs and guns and the wide sky; here it was like an Irish wolfhound in a terraced house. She stayed in the garden for a long time. She felt like she would never be hungry again even though lunch-time was well past. Cal came looking for her.

"Don't you want anything to eat?" he asked.

"Not just at the moment."

"Must you hate Trevor quite so much?"

"What makes you say that?"

"I don't know what he said to

enrage you but the look you gave him would have fried eggs. Hate is very debilitating."

"It's very what?"

"I mean it. Stop hating him. There are better ways to spend your time."

"I don't know how to. I've been this way for so long."

"Look, if Trevor is killed in a car accident tomorrow you'll be psychiatric material. Let up, will you?"

"You don't understand."

"What don't I understand?"

Mary didn't say anything. Cal looked keenly at her, like he looked when somebody was trying to better him at work. Then he put an arm around her and walked her slowly across the lawns to the pretty green summerhouse which was all shabby wood and shaded seats. He sat her down there, still with an arm around her on the old sofa and he said softly against her hair, "Tell me about it."

"I can't."

Cal drew her into his arms, against

his shoulder and stroked her hair. "Just close your eyes and tell me about it. Go on, just a little."

So she did, but quite haltingly at first, because she had never told anyone except Susan, because Cal was a man and because to speak the words outside seemed to give them permanence.

"I was very pretty when we were first married and he was very jealous and I had to be careful. It was strange. He didn't encourage me to wear pretty clothes to make me look good. I think he liked me best when I was pregnant, when I wasn't available to other men. I mean I wasn't ever available. I thought I loved him. He didn't like me to look nice, that's all and if I did he used to get very angry and he used to hit me. Not much, you know, just slaps on the arms and round the ear and . . . " Mary started to cry softly. "I had cared for him. I mean I . . . in the end I didn't have to do anything for it. I wasn't to go out, I wasn't to talk to anybody. It was like being in gaol. The day before he left, it was the day before my birthday and I met this friend. I'd gone into town because Trevor said he would be away and my mother had the children. He was an old boyfriend and he drove me home. That was all. When I got into the house Trevor was there. He'd telephoned and I wasn't at home.

"I ran around the house to get away from him and Trevor smashed things, ornaments, cups, a vase. The bathroom was the only room that locked. I stayed in there until the next morning, my birthday and he was waiting for me. The house was a mess. He said I'd encouraged other men, gone to bed with them, he was going to leave me. It was all my fault. Kathy believed him. She listened to him and was kind to him and she was pretty. She dressed well and had a good job . . . and he hit me before he left. He hit me. I don't ever want to be near anybody again. I don't want to live with anybody. I — "

"Why didn't you tell me?"

"I couldn't. I couldn't tell anybody. I hate him. I can't stop hating him. He hates me. He must have hated me to treat me like that. You mustn't tell anybody. My parents don't know. I couldn't leave him, I had two children and no money and nowhere to go."

"He left you," Cal said.

"Yes. Then I learned how strong I was, what I could do, what I could achieve, what I can still do, always. I don't have to stay with any man, I can always leave. I've said that to myself over and over since I met you. I can leave you. I can walk out of here tomorrow and though I'd be sorry, I'd be all right. It was the children, you see. I couldn't let Trevor have them. He doesn't hurt them, if I thought he did then I'd do something about it but he hasn't ever laid a hand on them. I've always been the one who's had to come the heavy parent. Trevor liked hitting me. He liked it a lot."

Cal frowned for a moment or two and then got up.

"Where are you going? Cal?"
Mary shot after him.
"You can't. If you do anything he won't buy the house."
"Who cares?"
"I do. I do for four hundred and fifty thousand pounds. Cal, wait." She planted herself in front of him and put up both hands. "You didn't know me then. It's past. Kathy probably doesn't even know about it. She's pregnant. Cal, don't."
"Look what he's done to you. You don't care about me, you can't, can you?"
"You don't know."
"No, I don't. I don't think you've told me the bloody half."
"I wouldn't have said anything at all if I thought you'd react like this. I wanted you to understand."
"Oh, I understand, all right. I understand a whole lot."
Mary got hold of his arms as Cal tried to move her.
"He's my children's father. Please.

They don't know. Please, Cal, don't. It won't make any difference, even if you kill him it won't. Cal, please."

Cal stopped. "Then I'm going to ring him and tell him he can't have the house."

"If you do that it'll cost fifty thousand pounds. You said it isn't worth more than four hundred thousand on the open market. You're right, you're always right about things like that. You can't afford to make telephone calls that cost you fifty thousand."

"How can you look at things so coldly?"

"I learned. I had to. Men do it all the time. You do it, usually. You've just lost your temper, that's all. I'll make a nice lunch and we can have some wine and it'll be all right."

"It isn't all right."

"So it isn't, but at least you understand now," and Mary walked back across the lawn and into the house.

7

CAL was more than a little surprised to see his father that Monday morning. It had been one of the worst weekends of his life. His business was draining away, the woman he loved was not in love with him and he had sold the only thing which was keeping her near him, a pretty stone house with a slate roof. His dreams were tortured with Trevor hurting her, with Trevor taking the children, with Trevor smashing up the house. It was even a relief to go the office where they could make general conversation to each other but even here emotion was running high. Almost as high as his debts.

Cal hadn't seen his father for months. They didn't like each other. It was a mutual, almost comfortable thing. His father had avoided him for the first seven years of his life and sent him to boarding-school after that. Cal, now, couldn't blame him much. His parents were old when they had him and he was not a good child. He set the garage on fire when he was four, burning his father's new car. He flooded the entire downstairs of the house when he was five. He was too clever for them, too fast. His father couldn't even catch him to thicken his ear. He was brilliant at school and consequently bored stiff, spending a lot of time in the local pubs when he got older, so that he become an expert at snooker.

He got himself thrown out for smoking and drinking, started up in business, married the first girl who wouldn't go to bed with him and appalled all his family's respectable friends by living in a bad area and spending so much time bedding his wife that he neglected and consequently lost his business. It had been a lot of years since then, but his parents still saw him as difficult and he supposed he was. When he went home his father ignored him and his mother was rude to him. Now his father, well-dressed, looked sheepish. He was unsmiling.

"Nigel," Cal greeted him, "how are you?" He knew his father hated the use of his name, hated the apparent disrespect but he couldn't help himself.

"Is that her?" His father waved a neat trilby at the closed door.

"Yes, that's Mary. Would you like a proper introduction?"

"She told me who she was. At least she told me what her name was. Very pretty. Not stupid either."

"No, she's not that. Have a seat. I hope you haven't come to borrow any money. I'm a bit strapped for cash."

"Tom said. Not getting any better?"

"No."

"They always say it's economically sound for people to go bankrupt. Stops things getting out of hand. Inevitable too, the way things have been. Banks loaning too much, companies getting too big, inflation the way it is, people spending too much."

"Well, that's a comfort."

His father eyed him from weary blue orbs.

"Tom says it isn't your fault."

"It's not my fault I'm called Fitzgerald either but it won't make any difference. Come here to bale me out, have you?"

"No, I haven't. My money's invested and there it stays. I understand you're selling your house. Couldn't you have kept the house out of it?"

"I could have, yes. I'm sure economically you would have said it was the best way."

"Possibly. Where are you going to live?"

"I don't know."

"Nearest council estate?"

"It's not quite that bad."

"Mary has two children. What about them? Do they have a father to go to?"

"Yes, they have a father to go to," Cal said, not looking at him.

"Like that, is it? Got a suggestion to put to you. Why don't you come and live with us?"

Cal nearly fell off his chair.

"What?"

His father waved both arms.

"Six bedrooms, three bathrooms, half-a-dozen downstairs rooms like bloody garages. Ten acres. Your mother and I, we're not exactly crushed."

"Why don't you sell it if it's too big?"

"I didn't say it was too big."

"Then why don't you ask Tom?"

"He likes his own house. I offered to swap him years ago but he wouldn't."

"Dad, I haven't changed. You didn't like living with me."

"You were impossible," his father said.

"I'm still impossible."

"Mary lives with you."

"It wasn't her choice. It was necessity. Their father tried to take them. The children are small and boisterous. I don't think you'd like it. We row too.

We shout. Just think what your friends would say."

"I'm thinking what my friends will say when you're bankrupt and bloody well homeless." His father glanced at him and then said gruffly, "Are you going to marry her?"

"No."

"Why not?"

"That's our business."

His father got up.

"I'm going. It's too nice a day for staying in an office. Think about it. It seems to me that your mother would like Mary."

My God, Cal thought, she's made an impression on the old man.

The following day his mother telephoned.

"Bring Mary to dinner on Saturday evening," she said. "Eight for half-past."

"My parents have invited us to dinner on Saturday," Cal told her as they drove home.

Mary looked hard at him, eyes wide.

Cal wasn't surprised.

"I thought you didn't get on with them."

"I don't."

"Then why have they invited us for dinner?"

"My father liked you."

"But I only saw him for two minutes. Do we have to go? I suppose we do. Whatever will I wear? Will there be other people?"

"Tom and Annabel."

"Thank goodness for that," and the minute they reached home Mary telephoned Annabel to ask what she was wearing.

★ ★ ★

His parents lived on the edge of the most prestigious village in the area. The houses were all different, many of them old with big gardens and wide gates. The house itself was old and built in an L shape and was white with a tiled roof. It had big gardens around it. There was a big drive up to one side of the property and then to the back and to one side were the remaining eight-and-a-half acres.

Mary was nervous. Tom's car was already parked outside which made her feel a bit better. Annabel smiled encouragingly at her when she went in but Mary soon lost her nervousness. Cal's parents, she thought, were lovely. His father fussed around her, gave her a glass of red wine, showed her his favourite paintings in the hall. Her mother called her 'my dear', the good smells from the kitchen confirmed Mary's hope that it would be an excellent dinner and it was. There was no shortage of conversation. Annabel and Tom were obviously frequent visitors. The only hitch to Mary's evening was the way that Cal said nothing. He ate and was polite but he didn't aid the conversation one little bit and Mary soon saw why. It was all Tom.

When his mother looked on Tom

her eyes shone. She asked all about the children, told Mary how wonderful they were, and Mary thought of Eileen and the child Cal didn't have and she couldn't eat the pavlova which Cal's mother had made so carefully. Their father called Tom 'my boy' and they talked about old times when Annabel and Tom were first married and about the children and about Nigel's work. They didn't talk about the chocolate company, about its successes or its problems. Emily did ask Mary about her children but the evening grew longer and longer until Mary couldn't wait to leave. Cal didn't speak a word all the way home and the first thing he did was to pour himself a generous amount of brandy. He took the glass and went out into the garden. Mary thought for a moment or two and then she followed him. The night was warm. He was leaning against a big tree at the far side of the garden.

"Why do your parents treat you like that?"

He turned slightly as she spoke and even smiled.

"Like what?"

"I don't know." Mary moved nearer. "Like you were illegitimate or adopted or worse. Are you?"

"What, worse? I expect so."

"What did you do?"

"Oh," Cal sighed, "just about everything. I was born awkward."

"I don't think you're awkward. I think you're a peach."

Cal laughed a little.

"No, you are. You're easy to work for, easy to live with, kind, generous, loving. You don't moan, you never throw your intellectual weight about — "

"I haven't any."

"No, of course you haven't. You're kinder to people than they are to you, though I suspect that's a sort of superiority on your part. You won't fight anybody who isn't up to your weight, which lets out just about everybody, but does that have to include your parents? They think less of you for it. They think it's weakness in you."

"I have enough trouble with what I think, never mind what other people think."

"You could open your mind for people just a little sometimes. They won't all frighten. How do they think you got to be chairman of a company at your age? Do they think you behave all the time like you did tonight? Don't they understand?"

"I expect it cuts both ways."

"There you go. Fob her off and give her the cliché. That isn't what you think at all. You forget. I see you at work. I sit in the office next door. You can't hide your mind all the time and it's not very courteous of you to do it either."

"I'm sorry. I can't think of a single brilliant remark. My parents want us to go and live with them."

"Live with them? Whatever for?"

"Because they have a great big house and we're about to sell ours."

"But they don't like you."

"Tom and Annabel don't want the house and my father doesn't want to get rid of it."

"Who told you this?"

"My father."

"It's a very nice house, Cal, but I don't think I could stand the way your parents treat you for a weekend, never mind for good."

"There's plenty of room." Cal said. "Did you like it?"

Mary looked stubbornly at him.

"No," she said. "I didn't like it one little bit."

"But you'll go and live there rather than let Trevor have the children."

"I don't need to answer that."

"OK." Cal finished his brandy. "Don't tell anybody."

"Why not?"

"Because if Trevor finds out he won't buy this place."

Mary looked at him. "What?"

"He thinks he's practically putting you on the street, that I won't be able to afford a decent house, that we may even split up and either way he will get the children. The children will have to change schools. Have you considered that?"

"They're the best schools in the area."

"Don't sound so smug."

"It's the only thing I'm in favour of. Will we have to eat with your parents?"

"We can go out to dinner a lot. They'll babysit."

"So they will," Mary said and cheered up.

★ ★ ★

Mary's children were a big hit with Cal's parents. She was quite surprised at that until she looked objectively at them. Both her children looked like her, they had blond, almost white hair and blue eyes and they were tanned golden from the summer sun.

Under Cal's influence and money

they were well-dressed and confident and because of her they were well-mannered and kind. They were also happy. They loved the new house. Mary enrolled them in new schools for the autumn term and they quickly made friends in the village and were out all day while the sun shone. Mary hadn't wanted to put on his parents and suggested childminders while she worked but Emily was horrified. She was delighted to have them. Mary didn't think it would work but since Cal's parents had help in the house and a gardener, with four adults and their friends her children spent a happy summer. Mary derived great satisfaction from telling Trevor where he could pick up the children his first weekend after they moved out of the town. He said nothing. The house was bought and paid for then.

Cal had been right about the house, there was a lot of room but even so he kept out of his parents' way and out of hers. He worked. He left early and came home late. If he was going to be there for the evening he arranged so that he could take her out but they tended to talk about work when they went out alone and that made Mary tense. But having dinner with Cal and his parents was no easier. His father's conversation tended to be about financial affairs, about the various firms which had gone bankrupt. He offered Cal all kinds of advice and he talked about successful men he knew. Cal's mother talked to him about Tom, Tom's wife, Tom's children, Tom's golf, Tom's ideas. Mary didn't think Emily knew she was doing it. Cal said little. He didn't argue, he didn't object, he didn't eat. He didn't sleep.

Cal got quieter and quieter until he could go a whole evening without speaking to anyone. They had their own sitting-room but he was never there. When he was at home he worked in the evenings and Mary awoke two nights running at four and the light was still on in his room, which was a very big room he used as an office as well as a bed. The second night she climbed out of bed and stole across the landing. When she opened the door Cal didn't even look up from where he was sitting at the desk. He looked up when Mary went and stood over him.

"Must you work?"

"If you want to go on eating."

"I'll cut out the smoked salmon and the caviare if it means you can go to bed."

"I'm not tired."

"Yes, you are. You're very tired. You'll start to make mistakes if you don't rest."

He laughed at that.

"Things can get worse?" he said.

"Why don't we go away for the weekend?"

"I haven't time."

"Aren't we going to have a holiday?"

"You're entitled to some time off. Take it."

"Will you please go to bed?"

"Yes. In a minute."

Mary gave up. Neither did she take much time off. He needed her there. It was nice to be so important to him at work but she felt guilty about the children and tried to spend her weekends with them. She took the odd day but work was so complicated now.

The new chocolates had been made and new advertising had been arranged and Cal was doing everything possible to make people want the products. One cool day when the sky was overcast and Mary was wishing herself anywhere but at work, there was a telephone call from a big chain store, someone they hadn't dealt with before. Shortly afterwards he came out of the office and got hold of her and hugged her.

"Yes?"

"Yes. Mike did that. I'm going to take him out to lunch. You coming?"

"I'm busy."

"Oh come on."

She hadn't seen him properly in days so Mary went and while Cal was still in a good mood after champagne Tom called in to his office.

"Annabel said are you coming to supper on Saturday night?"

"Of course we are," Cal said genially and it was not until he parked his car beside Trevor's Range Rover that Saturday evening that he considered there might be other people.

"Tom didn't say so."

"They're very good friends. We can't back out now."

Worse still, as they were getting out of the car Phil and Samantha Thompson arrived.

It was a lovely summer night. They gathered in the sitting-room with the french windows open and Cal wandered into the garden. When Mary looked up Samantha Thompson had wandered after him and they were talking softly and laughing. Mary tried to contain the way that she felt. Cal wasn't hers. She wouldn't let him touch her. But she was shaking.

She wanted to run into the garden

and throw a drink over Sam. She tried to concentrate on what Annabel was saying to her and followed Annabel into the kitchen. Annabel looked worried. Mary thought it was the dinner at first until Annabel turned to her.

"If you don't watch out you're going to lose him. You do know that, don't you?"

"It's very complicated, Annabel."

"It'll be a damned sight more complicated if Sam leaves Phil."

"Why did you invite them?"

Annabel looked patiently at her.

"Mary, Sam is one of my friends. I have lunch with her. Our children play together. It's time to decide what you want. They've already had an affair and she thinks she's in love with him. And he looks to me like someone who'd appreciate a good time. If she leaves Phil because Cal takes her to bed there's going to be the biggest mess."

"He's living with me."

"No. You're living with him, in his parents' house. You'll be the one who leaves. What the hell is going on? I thought he was in love with you. What happened?"

"He hasn't ever been in love with me, Annabel."

"Are you quite sure about that?" Annabel said. "Is it the responsibility of that that upsets you? Don't you really care about him or are you frightened to? You're going to have to find out and fairly quickly I would say."

Mary couldn't eat. She wandered upstairs after dinner when people scattered to help in the kitchen or to find brandy in the living-room and from the pretty stained-glass window half-way up the stairs she was nicely in time to watch Samantha Thompson smooth Cal's hair with one slim hand and put her mouth on his. They couldn't be seen from downstairs, a big tree was between them and the lawns beside the house. She stood there as Cal gathered Sam into his arms and then she went on up to the bathroom and splashed water over her face. They had gone by the time she came back and were in the sitting-room with Tom and Kathy and Trevor.

Mary got through the rest of the evening the best way that she could but even her coffee cup shook in her hands. They didn't speak during the drive back. His parents had gone to bed. Mary lingered in the kitchen but couldn't help following him into the drawing-room. The night was warm. He was standing by the open french window, silent and still.

"I watched you kissing Sam in the garden," Mary said.

He turned around and looked at her in surprise.

"Did you?"

"I was half-way upstairs."

"This isn't an objection surely."

"She has Phil's baby in her and I don't think he has any idea that his wife is in love with you."

"She isn't in love with me."

"Isn't she?"

"What the hell difference does it make to you anyway?" Cal walked out, into the garden and she went after him.

"You can't do that."

"Their marriage is dropping apart," Cal said patiently as she caught him up on the lawn.

"My marriage was dropping apart too but I didn't feel any better for having Kathy smash it like an old vase. Did you see them tonight? Did you see how Kathy looked? She has his babies too. Trevor doesn't love her. His second marriage is going the same way as his first but when things are in a very bad way like that, to have another man pretend that he cares for you so that you'll go to bed with him ... I don't know what I would have done."

"I'm not pretending that I care for her. I've never pretended that with anybody."

"That's not the point. You're more successful than Phil, you're younger and taller and — "

"What the hell does that have to do with it?"

"It just does."

"If Trevor had been a garden gnome it wouldn't have made any difference to you. You went to bed with me and spent the next six months pretending you hadn't, wishing you hadn't. Like you had something to lose."

"I had a lot to lose."

"Oh yes? Like what?"

"Like my job — "

Cal glared at her.

"Likely."

"Possibly. I didn't know you very well, did I? What if we'd had an affair and then it had ended? I need that job. I needed the money."

"There was never any question of that."

"There might have been. I had my independence to lose too. I lost that anyway. I gave that up for the children."

"Gave it up?" Cal repeated. "You

gave up a tatty little house in a bad area. That's all."

"Grey House was nearly all yours and this house belongs to your parents. None of it was anything to do with me and do you know what that means? It's called power."

"Well, a bloody long way it got me," Cal said and stormed off.

Mary watched him for a couple of minutes and then ran after him into the orchard.

"Cal, please." When he stopped and looked at her Mary found that her fists were clenched at her sides. "Don't do it. Please."

He got hold of her and pulled her into his arms and kissed her. Mary gave him her mouth and her arms and he tightened his hold on her. He kissed her all over her face and her neck and her shoulders. He kissed her and told her over and over how much he loved her. He drew her down into the warm grass and his hands gentled her. Mary could feel the grass, she could smell the fruit on the trees. The plum trees. The fruit trees, like the orchard in the country where she had lived with Trevor.

It was September. The plums were turning colour in the orchard, the days were golden. It was a golden day, the day before her birthday and she had come home, the old boyfriend, he was called Mark, had left her there. The next day was to be her birthday. She was standing in the orchard when she heard Trevor's car and then he was there among the plum trees and he was shouting at her. Trevor had never seemed so big, so frightening. She tried to get around him, she tried to get past him but she couldn't.

Trevor was bigger than she was, he liked being bigger than she was, he liked being stronger than she was. He hit her, like it was play, a tiny stinging slap over the ear so that she put up both hands. He flicked his fingertips over her other ear in the same way.

"Don't."

She tried to get past him but he had hold of her.

"Don't."

She jerked free and ran, over the warm grass, over the lawn, with Trevor just behind her. She ran into the house and through the kitchen and up the stairs and managed to get the bathroom door closed just in time. She stayed there with her back against the door and the night drew in. She wasn't hungry, she felt sick. After a long time she fell asleep and awoke to hear a car.

It was very early in the morning of her birthday. Slowly she unlocked the door. In the shadows of the hall Trevor was waiting for her. She gave a cry and tried to turn away but he wouldn't let her. He shouted at her and swore at her. The hall was narrow and she couldn't get away from him. The hall was narrow and there were shadows because it was dark early morning and there was rain. She backed into the door of the playroom and it burst open and she tripped over a toy and fell. Trevor was so big. Trevor was so near, his face and his hands, and his fingers digging into her. Trevor lifting her up, she fighting with him, Trevor holding her still, hitting her methodically, the room full of the sound of his hands on her. She cried out.

Cal let go. She lay face down in the sweet orchard grass, breathing heavily.

"Don't touch me."

"I'm not."

"I don't want you to touch me."

"I'm not," he said again.

"I don't want you to touch me ever again, not ever. I can't love you, not you and not anybody. Don't touch me. Go away."

She didn't open her eyes until she heard the sound of the car dying away down the drive, until it halted there and then went forward again. When the sound of it was finally gone she got up and walked slowly back to the house. In bed, in the dark the tears wouldn't even come.

8

IT was late when she awoke the following morning, after eleven. There was something strange about the house, it was so quiet. She put on a dressing-gown and ventured downstairs. She saw the children playing in the garden. When she opened the kitchen door they all looked up, Emily, Nigel and Tom. Emily and Nigel were seated at the table and Tom was standing by the cooker.

"What is it?" she said. "What's wrong?"

They looked at each other.

"It's Cal," Tom said flatly, "he's in gaol."

She looked at Cal's parents but both of them looked down.

"Trevor's in hospital," Tom said.

Mary glanced out of the window to where her children were running around the garden, shrieking and laughing with four of their friends.

"Is Trevor badly hurt?" she said.

"He has a broken nose, several cracked ribs and either one black eye or two, Cal couldn't quite remember. I think he was hoping it was two."

Mary stood by the door for a few seconds longer and then she said, "I think I'd better go upstairs and pack. Excuse me."

Emily got up and went to her, put an arm around her. "We don't want you to do that. Nigel, pour some tea."

Mary shook her head. "You're very kind but I can't stay. It was my fault. I told him I didn't want him. I was frightened. I'm frightened." She put both hands over her face. Emily guided her to the table and sat her down. "I shouldn't have told him about Trevor, only he's so persuasive. I didn't think he would connect it up like that. That's what comes of being too bright for your own good. What on earth was he doing? As though that would make any difference. What will happen when the newspapers find out?" Mary lifted her wet face to Tom's gaze. "We've been in the papers so much lately. It's bound to come out and my parents don't know. They don't know that Trevor . . . "

"Don't you think you ought to have told them?" Emily asked gently.

"I couldn't. I wasn't going to tell anybody. I wouldn't have told Cal but . . . "

"You told him last night?" Tom asked.

"No, months ago. Last night . . . I think he wanted me to make some kind of commitment, he sort of forced my hand and I . . . I'm just not ready to. I can't stay here, it isn't fair to you, it isn't fair to Cal either."

Nigel coughed as though he had rehearsed.

"We want you here," he said, "we want the children too."

"You don't want Cal."

"We do," Emily said. "We do care

for him very much, it's just that Calum is so . . . so difficult to love."

"No, he isn't," Mary said. "He's the easiest person in the world to love; he just chooses the wrong people to give his affection to, it's his only fault, that and not being able to hurt people to save himself."

They were looking blankly at her. Mary walked out of the kitchen. She was half-way up the stairs when she heard Tom's voice.

"Mary . . . " He followed her and for the first time Mary saw the resemblance between the two brothers. "Don't you think the children have been pulled about enough? What can it hurt if you stay here?"

"If I stay then Cal can't."

Tom smiled politely.

"I doubt he has any intention of doing so."

"Your parents have got to show Cal that they want him. If they don't they'll lose him," and Mary continued on her way up the stairs.

★ ★ ★

The story hit the newspapers the following day, and Mary went to see her parents.

"You can stay with us," her mother offered.

"I don't know what I'm going to do but just for the next few days I'll stay with Susan. Peter's away and the children can play together."

Her mother hugged her. Her father said, "You should have told us, you know."

"There was nothing you could have done."

"Why didn't you leave him, Mary?" her mother asked.

"I didn't want people to know."

★ ★ ★

Mary went to work as usual on the Monday morning, though her hands trembled when she walked into the office and the lights were on in Cal's room, it being a rainy day. She went to the door and peeped in. Tom was sitting at Cal's desk. He looked up.

"You see before you the acting chairman," he said.

"Where's Cal?"

Tom looked straight at her. "I don't know where he is, Mary. He just told me to manage things for a while so I said I would."

Mary nodded. "I can't give you my notice yet because I don't have another job to go to but I will find one this week."

"That isn't necessary — "

"I think it is. Will you give me a reference?"

Mary had a busy week. She went looking for work, she went searching for a house. By Friday she had found a house to rent, she thought that would give her some space in which to look for the right place to live. A job took rather longer to find. That weekend was Trevor's weekend for having the children but nobody contacted her. Mary drank a full bottle of red wine that Saturday night and slept well. When she went in on the Monday morning Tom called her into the office.

"I've got you an interview," he said.

"You have?"

"A job with more money. How's that?"

"More money?"

"Slightly more, not much."

"That would be wonderful, Tom. Where?"

"Just up the road. Paul Archer is looking for a secretary."

"Is he married?"

"No."

"Is he old?"

"No."

"Are you sure it's a good idea?"

"It's more money. He's older than Cal."

Paul Archer was about four years older than Cal, Mary estimated, which didn't get him much nearer his pension. In a lot of ways it was like working for Cal even though the product was different; Archer's made shoes. He was competent like Cal, worked hard, knew how to delegate and cared. On the Friday of her first week there Annabel and Tom had invited her to supper. As Mary parked her car outside the house Tom came out to her.

"We didn't do this on purpose, Mary, but my brother's here. He arrived about ten minutes ago and I didn't like to turn him away. He says if you object he'll go."

"I don't object," Mary said trembling. "I just wish he hadn't hit Trevor, that's all."

She locked the car and went inside with Tom. It was several weeks since she had seen him. Cal was thinner. He was very tanned as though he had been away, wearing a white shirt which accentuated the tan, blue jeans and sneakers. He looked about ten years younger than Paul Archer, Mary decided, the straight dark shiny hair and smoky grey eyes. She had a terrible desire to ask him when he had last eaten properly. Above all he looked as though he hadn't hit anybody in his life but Mary had had full details of Trevor's injuries and wasn't deceived.

"Hello, Cal," she managed, "how are you?"

"I'm fine. I hear you went to Archer's for more money."

"It seemed like the best thing to do."

Annabel kissed her and offered her a drink. Tom went for the drinks, Annabel to attend to the meal.

Cal said nothing. It reminded Mary of the evenings spent with his parents.

"Are you still at home?"

"No." Cal looked up from where he had settled by the fire. "I haven't been back. Where are you living?"

Mary sat down in the chair opposite.

"I found a rented house."

"What's Archer like to work for?"

"Rather like you except that he doesn't beat up my ex-husband." Mary hadn't intended to say that. She hadn't realized that she was still angry.

Cal didn't look up. "I'm sorry," he said.

"You didn't think, did you, about how I would feel or the children, or my parents or Kathy, or what it would be like when everyone knew?"

"No. I didn't," Cal's voice was low.

"All you thought about was the way that you felt. All you thought about was your frustration and you vented that frustration on Trevor. How could you?"

"You make it sound like the way that I felt meant nothing," Cal said.

"It hurt so many people."

He looked at her across the fire.

"It hurt so many people to find out what Trevor had done to you? That your husband beat you? You think people shouldn't know things like that?"

"It was nothing to do with you."

"No?" Cal's eyes had darkened. "It was fine for you to go to bed with me when there was no danger of commitment but you couldn't do it when we were living together. What are you going to do, spend the rest of your life having one-night stands? How do you think I felt all that time not being able to touch you?

"You knew that from the beginning. You knew I wasn't going to let you near me."

Cal shook his head. "I thought it was just a matter of time. I didn't know what had happened. You weren't going to tell anybody. We'd made love already, several times. I thought it was going to work out, I thought you were just nervous because your marriage hadn't been good."

"And finding out that my marriage had been violent what did you do? You behaved violently. Do you seriously think that I'd trust you? You put a man into hospital."

"That's the whole trouble," Cal said, eyes firing, "to you all men are like Trevor."

"You had no right to hit him."

"So I had no right to hit him but at least he was as big as me, as strong as me. Trevor had a chance. What chance did you have?"

Mary got to her feet.

"It was still none of your business," she said. "I don't want to listen to this. I'm going."

"Don't bother," Cal said and he opened the door just as Tom came back with a tray of drinks.

Tom put down the drinks and followed him.

"You rowed already?" he asked, following Cal to his car.

"It was a waste of time. I should have known it would be," Cal said, getting in and slamming the door.

"Did you think she wasn't upset about it?" Tom asked through the open car window.

"She just can't accept that Trevor is a bastard. She thinks everybody's like that. Well, I've had enough. I'm going to go out and find somebody who wants me," and Cal started up the car and tore down the drive.

Tom went back inside. Mary was sitting white-faced with a glass of red wine in her hand. "He thinks he's the only person in the whole world," she said tightly and she couldn't look up at Tom because her eyes glinted with tears.

Tom sat down and put an arm around her.

"My brother isn't good at losing," he said. "You'll have to give him some time to get used to it."

★ ★ ★

The following evening Mary had just put her children to bed when the doorbell rang. She passed the window on the way to the door and there stood Cal's white Mercedes. She hesitated and then opened the door. Cal was dressed rather as he had been last night except that the evening was chilly and he had on a black sweater as well.

"I just came to say I was sorry."

"Come in, but quietly, I've just put the kids to bed."

Cal was in the house only seconds, standing in the narrow hallway before the children realized who it was and came yelling down the stairs, throwing themselves at him. He picked them both up and hugged them and then he carried them back up the stairs, put them into bed and read them a story. When they settled down he walked down into the tiny living-room. Mary had the fire burning.

"More tatty than the other house, isn't it?" she said.

"I rather like it. It's on the edge of town. It has a good view of the hills from the back and you can have a real fire."

"Would you like a drink?"

"I haven't come to bother you. I just felt like a louse."

"I don't have any whisky. How about coffee?"

"Coffee's fine."

He followed her into the even smaller kitchen while Mary filled the kettle. "I miss the children."

"I think they miss you."

"Are they seeing Trevor?"

Mary shook her head.

"After all the fuss he used to make he hasn't been near. At least he'd have problems trying for custody of them now that people know. I don't know whether to be pleased that I don't have to put up with him or sorry because the children seem to have lost their father."

"Maybe I could come and take them out, that's if we can still be friends."

"That would be nice," Mary said.

They sat by the fire and drank coffee and began talking almost accidentally about work. He asked questions about her new job and she found that she was telling him all about Paul Archer and the shoe business, the problems and the stories. It was eleven o'clock before Mary noticed again.

That Saturday Cal came over and took the children out for the afternoon. Mary had a blissfully quiet few hours by the fire, reading a book and trying to forget all the housework she had to do. She asked Cal to stay and eat with them but he left hurriedly, saying, "Thanks but I have a dinner date. See you."

Mary pretended that she wasn't interested whom he was seeing but it was of little comfort when Susan called by the following afternoon.

"Guess who I saw in town with a blonde last night?" she said when the children had gone off to play.

"Pretty?"

"Very. Young too, not more than about twenty. Long hair, the kind of legs that go on forever. She was wearing a dress I'd have given years of my life for."

"At least it wasn't Samantha Thompson."

"She couldn't. She's as big as a house end. I heard it's twins. That'll keep her out of worse action for a while."

Mary sat by the fire, stared into the flames and didn't say anything.

"What will you do when he falls in love with somebody else?"

"I don't know."

"He will."

"Yes, I expect so."

"Men don't wait around, not like us, and it's not as if he's short, fat, ugly and broke, is it?"

Mary smiled into the fire.

"No," she said.

But the next time he telephoned to ask if he could take the children out Mary refused. That night when the children were fast asleep and she was sitting by the fire the doorbell rang and when she opened the door Cal was standing there.

"I couldn't talk to you from work," he said, following her inside and shutting the door. "What is going on? Why can't I see the children?"

"You're beginning to sound like

Trevor," Mary complained from the fireside.

"You think everything else about me is like him, so what?"

"I don't think that at all — "

"Every time I tried to take you into my arms you thought I was Trevor."

"Must we talk about it?"

"I came to ask you why I can't see the children. What earthly reason could you have for not letting me?"

"They're not yours."

"That's a reason?"

He looked puzzled. Mary turned around from the fire.

"Cal . . . Trevor goes in and out of their lives. I don't want them to think that all men do that — "

"It's your choice," Cal said shortly.

"It isn't my choice. That's not fair, Cal. I couldn't help it."

"Do you know what your trouble is?" Cal said. "You didn't try. You were that used to being a victim you couldn't be anything else. When we quarrelled you thought I was going to hit you. You expected it. It didn't occur to you that I'd never done such a thing, that I cared about you — "

"Yes, it did," Mary stopped him but she couldn't look at him, "it was just that it happened exactly like that that last time, on my birthday. I had spent all night waiting for him to go away and when I finally managed to get free I ran out of the house. It was exactly the same almost to the day. He ran after me into the orchard, the smell of the fruit trees ... and he got hold of me and he told me that he loved me ... I couldn't manage it, don't you see?"

"How was I meant to know this?"

"You weren't meant to, and there is no place for you in my children's life — "

"That's not fair," Cal said quickly, "they like me and I miss them. Just because you can't stand men that's no reason to deprive them of my company."

Mary looked coolly at him.

"Why don't you go away and find yourself a nice girl and have some of your own?" and she went across and opened the outside door for him.

9

TOM had got tired of leaving messages on the Ansaphone. It had been switched on for days. His parents were away and he thought that Cal was either away too or there was a good reason why he had not made contact. It was a cold evening when he drove across to the house. He parked the car and rang the doorbell several times before he heard soft noises inside and when the door opened a tall blonde girl stood there. She was young, with large blue eyes. She wore a lot of make-up, her eyes the larger for that, her mouth kissable. She also wore a dressing-gown which was open at the front and the kind of underwear which Annabel wore when she was eager to get him to make love to her, thin straps and shiny material and not much of it, outlining the fullness of her breasts and the slightness of her waist and the tops of her thighs.

"I'm Tom Fitzgerald," he said coolly. "May I come in?"

"Be my guest," she said smiling, "the whisky's all gone though."

Tom walked in.

"Where is he?"

The girl helped herself to a cigarette from his father's silver box.

"Upstairs. I shouldn't bother if I were you," she added as Tom set off in that direction, "he's had an awful lot to drink and if I can't wake him I doubt you can."

Tom went upstairs to Cal's room. The window was open, the room was freezing. He closed the window and switched on a bedside lamp. He sat down on the bed.

"Cal? Cal?" When there was no answer he shook Cal's bare shoulders.

Cal rolled over and opened his eyes just a touch.

"What the hell do you want?" he said. "Did a factory burn down?"

"Who is that girl?"

"What girl? Oh. She's called Pauline."

"What is she doing here? Are you paying her?"

Cal opened his eyes a little wider and laughed. His teeth looked so white against several days' dark stubble.

"Please," he said. "I met her at a party."

"She's isn't a prostitute?"

Cal grinned. "Depends how you look at it," he said. "She works in the City. That's her Ferrari outside. She brought me home."

"I want to talk business to you but I couldn't contact you and you're obviously in no fit state. Will you come to the office tomorrow?"

"Eight o'clock, sharp," Cal said, before turning back to the pillows.

"In the evening presumably," Tom scorned.

But when he reached the office at several minutes past eight the following morning his brother was already there, a little pale but sober, clean-shaven and wearing a dark blue suit.

"So," he said, "what's the problem?"

Tom dumped his overloaded briefcase on the floor beside the desk.

"The problem is the chairman isn't here."

"Can't you handle it?"

"How much longer?"

Cal got up, pushed his hands into his pockets.

"Bored?" he asked.

"No, you're the one who's bored. Your enthusiasm for this place walked out with Mary Dickinson."

Cal didn't answer.

"You can't go on like this, drinking yourself stupid and sleeping with every damned blonde you meet."

"I'm not."

"No? That's how it looks. She doesn't care about you, Cal, why can't you accept that? You were never anything more to Mary than a way out of a situation that she found impossible. You said yourself she had to do it to keep the children. That's what she did. She kept her children and she doesn't want you. She doesn't want you and she doesn't want you near her children. I know ... I know it's difficult because of what happened before but you don't have any option. You don't have any way out of it and getting drunk and taking to bed women who look like her isn't going to make the situation any better."

"I didn't," Cal said.

"Well, that's how it looks."

"She brought me home because I was drunk. I didn't sleep with her."

"I don't believe you. The other thing is you can't stay there. Mother and Dad are due home tomorrow. Come and stay with us."

Cal said nothing for a moment or two and then he looked up.

"Get your fat backside off my desk," he said.

★ ★ ★

The following evening Tom went home alone. Annabel met him at the door.

"Wouldn't he come? she said.

"I don't think he's speaking to me. At least he's at work. People haven't half scattered since yesterday morning. You've got to hand it to him he knows what he's doing. The place doesn't run the same and I hate his job. He can't go home. He'll probably go to a hotel."

Annabel put the children to bed. Tom read them a story. They had dinner. It grew late. They finished clearing up.

"I'm going to go and see if he's still there," Annabel said.

"It's late."

"I want to."

"I'll go."

"No. Let me."

"Annabel, it's late."

"I have a car-phone. I'm quite safe. Don't suffocate me, please," and Annabel put on a coat and left.

The light was still burning in the front entrance, the security men greeted her happily. She went quietly up the stairs, her shoes soft on the carpets as she made her way to his office. Cal wasn't working and he didn't hear her. He was standing by the window, jacket and tie off, with a glass of whisky in his hand.

"Isn't it a dreadful view?" Annabel said and he turned slightly and laughed.

"It's my favourite view," he said.

Annabel went over and joined him there and she looked out at the dimly-lit yard, the buildings, the vans, the lorries.

"Why didn't you have an office at the front of the building?"

"I like it best here."

"Must you drink whisky on an empty stomach?"

"Don't start, Annabel. You should have heard the lecture I got yesterday. I had to stop myself from thumping Tom."

"He was concerned about you."

"He just couldn't do my bloody job, that's all."

"Ain't it the truth though?" Annabel said. "I made beef stew for supper."

Cal put down the whisky glass.

"Tell me, Annabel, if I come back with you will you sleep with me?"

Cal got hold of her arms with fingers that gripped, brought her to him and kissed her hard on the mouth. Annabel put her arms around his neck and gave him her mouth and then he let go just sufficiently and she put one hand into his hair and Cal buried his face against her neck. Annabel held him in her arms for a long time.

"You don't have to keep pretending to Tom and me that everything's all right," she said, "or that whisky and blondes and work are going to make up for it. I know how you feel about her. I know very well."

"Oh, Annabel, what am I going to do? Why can't I handle it?"

"You're not meant to handle it. You're meant to allow yourself to be upset and angry and hurt and whatever else you need to be. Will you give yourself a break? Stop being so wonderful, nobody but your parents ever expected you to be perfect, look where it got them, and get yourself a name on the office door, you're not God."

Cal laughed against her hair.

"That's better," Annabel said.

"Do you think Mary felt like that?"

"Very likely. If Tom went on like you I'd feel obliged to turn out gourmet dinners and go to aerobics classes four times a week. Now are you coming home with me? Tom was opening a bottle of Medoc as I left and if we don't hurry he'll have drunk it all."

★ ★ ★

Mary worked hard at being happy; she desperately wanted some peace. For a while she didn't care for anything but work and to be with the children.

Trevor no longer came to see the children. Several times she almost rang Cal and apologized and told him that she did want the children to see him, the truth was that as the days went by she missed him, the children missed him, the little house became almost oppressive. She didn't go out. She was pleased not to go out at first but the nights were long and dark now, the children could not play outside and in the darkness the house was shabby, cold. Michael Addison had rung her several times but Mary refused to see him. Christmas was approaching again; she felt more trepidation than ever before. In November Paul Archer's engagement fell through.

"I think she just got tired of my working so much," Paul told Mary. "She's going to marry a teacher. Can you imagine that?"

"Teachers work hard too."

"At least they get decent holidays."

In early November Paul had to attend a number of social functions.

Awkwardly he asked Mary if she would go.

"I'm not asking you to do anything unprofessional and I won't get clever if you say no but I have got to go and I need somebody to go with me. Better still, I need somebody who knows what I'm talking about. I'll buy you some clothes and I'll pay you by the hour."

"You will not," Mary said hotly, "you pay me very well."

In a way it was a good social life for a week or two. She went to dinner dances with him, enjoyed the food and the dancing without the complication of a relationship. Then came the night when they stopped outside the area's most prestigious hotel and she saw Cal's Mercedes parked. Mary took several deep breaths before she went inside. The first person she saw was a tall slender blonde girl wearing a lovely silver dress. She was almost as tall as Cal. They were talking and laughing with another couple. Cal saw her and waved as though there was nothing wrong and later he came across to their table and introduced the blonde girl, Greta. Paul, always sociable, asked them to sit down, began talking to Greta and asked her to dance. Cal didn't ask Mary to dance. He didn't talk to her either. He watched as Paul waltzed the girl efficiently about the floor.

"I'd like to dance," Mary said finally.

Cal said nothing. He got up and they went on to the floor and he held her just as lightly, just as politely as she had seen him do with countless other women he was obliged to dance with when they had gone to similar events.

"How are Annabel and Tom?"

"Fine."

"And your parents?"

"They've gone to the south of France for the winter. My mother hasn't been well. They're talking about buying a house there."

"How's work?"

"Things are going very well just at present."

The music stopped but Paul and Greta stood talking until it started up again, which it did almost immediately. Soft, slow music. Cal took her into his arms but very carefully. Mary didn't know until then how much she had missed him. She missed living with him, having him around, feeling complete with the children. She missed talking about work, she missed the excitement and the problems. That was it. Her life was dull now. She was just Paul Archer's secretary whereas she knew now that Cal had never treated her like a secretary, she had always mattered to him. He had told her all the things about the company, which had made her feel important, he had included her in the exciting aspects of his life, the problems and the triumphs, and he had been there for her to lean on. Now there was no one to lean on, no one to talk to, no one to help and no one to put her first. Nobody special.

Paul and Greta came back to the table laughing and talking.

When Paul took her home at the end of the evening Mary stood in the small cold house and listened to the silence. Her children were with her parents, the house was empty.

10

THAT Thursday morning Cal's secretary, Elena, put a call through when he had said that he was taking no calls.

"What is it?" Cal said shortly.

"I have a little boy on the line, a very upset little boy. He says his name's Philip."

"Okay, put it through." Presently Cal heard a sniff and a bold,

"Is that you, Cal?"

"Yes, it's me. What's the matter?"

"I have to talk to you."

"Is something wrong?"

"I want to see you."

"Your mother doesn't want that. It's up to her."

"Vicky and I, we want to see you."

Cal closed his eyes.

"Phil, try to understand. I can't do that if your mother says no."

There was a short pause from the other end of the line and then, "Why don't you come and see us any more, don't you want to?"

"Yes."

"Then why don't you?"

"I can't until your mother says so."

"You don't want to see us — "

"Philip, I do."

"So when?"

"I'll talk to your mother about it."

"You promise?"

"Yes."

"If you don't come and see us soon we'll do something about it," Philip threatened and rang off.

★ ★ ★

She hadn't wanted Cal at her house. She left the children with Susan and went across to his parents'. It was early evening. When she drove through the town all the Christmas lights were burning and she thought of last Christmas, how much she had dreaded it. It had turned out to be a wonderful Christmas, a Christmas full of stars. She had gone to bed with Cal. They had spent Christmas Day at the seaside and it was a warm day and they had picnicked. Why couldn't you have a good day back again? Mary wondered. Why, when it had been as near to perfection as life ever was, could you not relive that day? She thought of the diamond earrings. She had been wearing the earrings at that dinner dance when she met Cal. Had he noticed that she wore them? Had he remembered how they had been in bed, how they had laughed, how he had kissed her on the neck, the earrings shining in the light?

She swung the car in to the drive. The outside light was burning at the front door and lamps were lit in the house. When she rang the bell Cal opened the door. He had changed into shirt and jeans when he came in from work. Some things didn't alter. Mary tried not to look into his eyes. She was afraid that he might know how much she wanted him.

"The children rang you at work?" she asked softly as Cal poured her a glass of red wine.

"Philip did, yes."

"That was very bad."

"It was very sensible. He could be sure of getting me there."

"What exactly did he say?"

"That they wanted to see me at Christmas."

"And what did you say?"

"I said it was up to you."

Mary stood by the fire.

"That puts me in a very difficult position, Cal."

"What the hell did you want me to say, that I didn't want to see them? Why should I? Why can't I see them?"

"I told you before." Mary turned around from the fire. "Trevor has gone out of their lives. First it was the divorce. Then it was all those moves. Then it was you. All these comings and goings. Whatever are they to think?"

"That life is unpredictable."

"I don't want that. I want stability for them."

Cal swore, softly and deliberately as he refilled his glass.

"They're entitled to that," Mary said.

"Entitled?" Cal glared at her. "What the hell is entitled? And stability is something you need on ships."

"Don't lecture me — "

"What is it, Mary? Do you want to be the only person your children care for?"

"Of course not — "

"I care about them. What is more important than affection?"

"Things which last — "

"Nothing lasts, for God's sake. Everything is transient. Children live in the present, and there's very bloody little wrong with that."

"Will you please stop swearing?"

"Oh, drink your wine and shut up," Cal advised.

Mary took a sip and then she watched

him because he wasn't looking at her. She liked how tall he was, how dark his hair was, eyes angry. Cal looked at her. Mary looked hastily down into her glass.

"Have you known Greta long?" she said.

"What?"

"The girl you took to the dinner dance?"

"Oh, yes. No, not long."

"She's very pretty."

"Yes."

"Paul liked her. When you talked to him you made it sound as though things were going very well at work."

"So?"

"They can't possibly be going that well."

Cal grinned. "Want my job?" he said.

"Seriously."

"Seriously . . . it's going to take a very long time. I'm broke."

"Oh, yes. All you have is a house with ten acres and a Mercedes."

"The house belongs to my parents. The car belongs to the firm."

"Won't it be all right?"

"It may be. I don't know yet. I just have to hope that nothing else goes wrong and work like hell. Are you going to your mother's for Christmas?"

"I expect so. At least this year Trevor isn't fighting to have the children for Christmas Day. What are you going to do?"

"Sleep."

Mary looked up and caught his eyes, felt the warmth hit her face and looked hastily around the room.

"You can see the children on Saturday if you like."

Cal thanked her and she finished her wine and left. She drove steadily back to the house, let the dog out the back and stood by the door, an icy wind blowing down the street, and she realized then that Cal would never again come to her. He would never voluntarily take her into his arms. As far as he was concerned they had not got past that day in the orchard when he had told her that he loved her. It would be a very long time, Mary thought, before he did that again, with anybody. He was cautious now. He was careful.

★ ★ ★

He was neither cautious nor careful the following Saturday when he arrived at the house but the children fell on him, shrieking and he got down to their level and gathered them to him. He took them out, bought them lunch, went with them to the cinema. When they came back in the darkness of early evening, he announcing that he must go, they clung and wouldn't let him out of the door. So he stayed and Mary made dinner. He took the children to bed, read them a story. When he walked slowly downstairs again Mary handed him a glass of whisky. Cal said, "Thanks," and slid on to the sofa with her by the fire.

"Are Tom and Annabel having the usual party on Christmas Eve?" Mary asked.

"Yes."

"How are they, if times are hard?"

"Oh, they're OK." Cal sat back and yawned. "Annabel was an only child. When her parents died they left her a lot of money. Would you like to come to the Christmas party?"

"No, thanks. I wasn't angling for an invitation."

"Trevor and Kathy won't be there this year."

"And Sam?"

"No." Cal gazed into the fire. "Everybody said it was a good party last year."

"Will you be going?"

"I'm supposed to show my face."

"Like you did last year?" Mary said, smiling. "You were only there ten minutes."

"Half an hour. I was there before you. You were wearing a black dress with a silver top."

"I couldn't afford it but I was glad I bought it."

"So was I."

"Cal..."

"Mm."

"Cal..."

This time he turned from the fire and looked at her.

"I'm sorry things didn't work out," Mary said.

"I'm sorry too."

When she went on looking at him Cal said, "I really have to go," and he got up.

★ ★ ★

Annabel telephoned and persuaded Mary to the Christmas party.

"There are going to be lots of people there that you know. They're always asking about you. It's not on Christmas Eve this year. That sort of cut into Christmas Day and the children are older this year so we're having the party on Boxing Day."

Mary let herself be persuaded and by the time Boxing Day arrived she was glad that she had done so. Her parents had been very kind but Christmas Day had been a big non-event. The children had enjoyed opening their presents. Mary had few to open. By the end of the day she was tired and the children were glad to go home and by the following evening, having spent Boxing Day alone with them, she was glad to drop them off at Susan's for the night and drive herself to the party.

It was so different from last year. She seemed to know everybody. She accepted a drink and went around talking to various people. She wore a different dress, another she had bought especially but not nearly as expensive; it was blue taffeta, quite plain. When it was late people stopped talking and began to dance. Mary decided it was time to go home. Tom asked her to dance. Mary was convinced he was being kind.

"It's late," she said.

"I thought you said the children were at your sister's. You don't have to get back."

So Mary danced with him and then she made the excuse again but then Cal asked her and she didn't like to refuse him. He took her into his arms and for Mary the magic happened all over again just as it had the Christmas before. She fought with the feelings but she and Cal went on dancing and the slow soft music made her think that she was back there. When she did decide it was time to go Cal offered to take her home and Mary was angry with herself for having a car. She didn't want to leave him. He walked her to her car and when they got there she turned to him and kissed him.

"You will be careful," Cal said.

"Yes."

She turned to the car and then hesitated. "I want you to come with me," she said.

Cal frowned in the streetlight.

"Are you nervous?" he said.

"No."

"The roads are dry. It's perfectly safe."

"No." Mary reached up and kissed him again. She put her arms around his neck. Cal hesitated and then he stopped her and said, "If you want me to go to bed with you why can't you just say it?"

"I thought I had. It isn't easy."

"No, it isn't, is it? Do you want to go to your house?"

"It's cold and dark there, Cal. The fire's been out for hours." They left her car. The magic wasn't gone but it was quite changed. She knew long before they reached his parents' house that Cal was not in love with her any more. She knew just by the way that he drove the car. He gave the driving his full concentration. He didn't talk to her. And even though they had not been in love that previous Christmas there had been laughter and fun and anticipation. There was anticipation here too but it wasn't the same.

The house was warm. Mary was already regretting the decision but when Cal closed the door he got hold of her and she stopped regretting it. They didn't go to bed. They got as far as the sofa. Mary knew that the next morning she was going to be angry with herself, not like she had been last time, very upset. Having turned Cal away when he had offered love she now was apparently content to have him rive off the minimum of her clothes to reach her body. Mary was horrified at herself. She couldn't remember having been as hungry in her life. And after that it was just greed, on the rug by the long-dead fire and in the warmth of his bed.

"You're bloody well insatiable, do you know that?" Cal said finally.

"Do you have any wine?"

"Alcohol as well? Yes, I have wine. Did you have anything particular in mind?"

"Champagne would be nice."

"Don't disturb yourself. I'll see what I can find."

There was no champagne but Mary was glad because they had claret instead and it warmed her and bread and pâté and cheese. She drank too quickly and was very happy by the time she fell asleep in his arms.

When she awoke it was half-past ten. She found a dressing-gown and tiptoed down the stairs. Cal was sitting in the kitchen, drinking coffee and reading the newspaper and when he looked up there was something in his eyes that she hadn't seen before. A look of blunt amusement.

"Sleep well?" he asked.

"Yes. Yes, thanks." Mary sat down in the nearest chair.

"Want some breakfast?"

"No, thanks. I'm not very hungry."

"What time are you picking the children up?"

"Not until tea-time."

"There's no hurry then. Have some coffee," and he poured a cup for her and slid it towards her. "Toast?"

"No. Cal, I'm sorry."

"Why sorry? Did somebody do something wrong? I like going to bed with you, didn't you notice?" Mary put both hands over her face and he got up and took hold of her and sat her down on his knees and put his arms around her.

"Will you stop getting upset? It was absolutely bloody perfect."

He kissed her neck several times and Mary put her arms around his neck and hid her face against him.

★ ★ ★

She waited for the telephone to ring. She waited a full week and then she went to bed and cried. After ten days Cal rang. He had been away. But it was the children he wanted to see. Mary asked him to stay when he brought them home but Cal said he couldn't and when Mary went into work on the Monday morning Paul Archer had been to a party on the Saturday night and Cal had been there with Greta.

It snowed the following week and Cal wanted to take the children sledging. Mary provided hot soup for when they came home and she asked Cal softly, "How's Greta?"

"She's fine."

"Paul said he'd seen you at a party."

"A party?" Cal looked up momentarily from his soup.

"Oh yes, I remember."

"Was it a good party?"

"Yes."

Cal waited until the children were in bed and then he followed her into the kitchen. He got hold of her arm and turned her to him.

"I am not sleeping with her. I never have slept with her and I have no intention of doing so."

"But you took her to a party."

"It was a business thing. There were several contacts I needed to make and as a matter of fact I like her. We're friends. You wouldn't have gone to the party with me."

"How do you know that?"

"I just do."

"I might have done."

"Mary, we've been through all that. You don't want a relationship. You chewed me up into little pieces and spat me out. You like going to bed with me and that's all. That was all it was from the beginning only I didn't understand that. I do now."

"That just isn't true. It was you, sleeping with Sam Thompson, and I was supposed to trust you. Well, I don't. It wouldn't surprise me to find that you are going to bed with Greta."

She broke away and after that there was a long silence during which Mary could have bitten out her tongue. She knew very well that it was jealousy talking and nothing more. She turned around but it was much too late.

Cal gave her one swift look and then he walked out of the house. The night was dark and rainy. Mary ran after him, shouting his name.

"Cal, I didn't mean it. Cal!"

Through the rain she watched the white Mercedes as it shot down the road.

★ ★ ★

Tom went to the telephone. Annabel was sitting by the fire making a sweater for her husband. He soon came back.

"Cal's had a car accident."

Annabel looked up as he put his hands on the back of the sofa.

"Is he hurt?"

"He sounds all right. Lost it on a roundabout in the rain, just missed a concrete post. I'm going to ring the garage and go and get him. I'll not be long."

Tom drove carefully. The rain was heavy. He picked Cal out with the car headlights, saw the white car show up easily. He stopped the car, got out.

"You've made a good job of that," he said, looking at the crushed bonnet.

"Just run me home, will you?"

"Going too fast?"

"Will you just drive, please," and Cal got into Tom's car and slammed the passenger door.

Tom said nothing else. He drove, carefully, back to his house.

"I didn't mean here," Cal said, as they got out.

"I know you didn't," his brother said calmly, "but I thought it was best."

"You thought." Cal glared at him through the rain.

"You're shaking," Tom said, "and it isn't all temper. Are you never going to learn? Driving like that in the rain. You could have hit that bloody post and been killed."

"I didn't hit it."

"You missed it by inches," Tom said, yelling, "a few inches. You bloody idiot."

Annabel put on the porch light and came to the door.

"Why don't you come inside and shout? It's drier," she said.

"My brother just tried to kill himself," Tom said from between his teeth.

"I did not."

"Thinking about that bloody girl, weren't you?"

"Tom, will you please stop swearing? We do have neighbours. We also have two children who are trying to sleep. Come inside. Tom, I mean now."

"You should see the car," Tom said hoarsely. He looked at Cal. "When are you ever going to give up on her? When?" He stood for another second and then pushed past Annabel into the house.

"I thought it was over," Annabel said softly.

"I love her. I have done since we met. I knew it wasn't going to be any good, right from the start. Trevor hurt her so much. She doesn't trust me at all. I wouldn't care only I haven't done anything wrong apart from hit Trevor."

"I'm not sure that was wrong," Annabel said.

"She was upset about Sam but that was all over before I met Mary."

"It was the idea of you sleeping with another man's wife," Annabel said.

"I know."

Annabel moved off the porch, into the rain. "I told you before, you're only almost perfect."

He smiled at that.

"Come on. You need a drink."

Cal followed Tom upstairs and his brother gave him some dry clothes. Downstairs again Annabel gave him a glass of whisky. Cal's hands shook. He sat down by the fire and after a little while Tom came downstairs and they all sat round, drinking whisky and talking slowly. After about an hour the doorbell rang and Annabel went to the door. Standing there in a cream mackintosh was Mary, her blonde hair a little darkened with rain.

"Is Cal here?" she asked.

Annabel came out on to the porch and closed the door.

"Yes, he's here," she said softly.

"He went off and I had to wake the

children and he wasn't at his parent's house and ... "

"He smashed up the car," Annabel said. "He's not hurt, just a bit shaken."

Tears drenched Mary's eyes. "It was my fault," she said.

"Mary ... if you don't care about him you've got to leave him alone — "

"I do. I do care."

"You've got to stop being frightened and accept that things won't always be great but that he isn't Trevor. You're going to have to give him a chance to prove that he isn't Trevor. If you don't care that much and you can't leave him alone he's going to end up in the direction he's been going for years. Nothing he's done has ever been enough for his parents and it never will be. Somebody has to believe that he's fine as he is. He doesn't believe it. He's spent his entire life not being Tom."

"But ... " Mary said and then stopped.

"Yes, I know that he's brighter than my darling husband but he doesn't believe any of it because he spent his childhood listening to how wonderful Tom was."

"Not just then," Mary said.

"I know. Now, you have got to give him a chance, Mary, or he's going to be the kind of man who lives his life for his work and ends up divorced all over the place and messed up — "

"Can I come in?" Mary said.

★ ★ ★

Cal looked accusingly at her when she was ushered into the living-room.

"What are you doing here?" he said.

"I was worried about you."

"Whatever for?"

"Annabel said you had an accident."

"It was just because the road was wet. You don't have to concern yourself about me. I'm fine," and he got up and walked out.

★ ★ ★

That week Cal took Greta out four times. He took her to the best restaurants, he took her dancing, he introduced her to influential people. On the fourth evening when he stopped outside her door Greta said, as she had said each time, "Are you coming in?" and for the first time Cal agreed.

He followed her into the kitchen and there she turned and looked at him so he kissed her. He put his arms around her and kissed her and went on kissing her. She responded and Cal kept waiting for it to get better. When it didn't he stopped.

"Greta, I'm sorry but — "

"I'm sorry too. Paul Archer has asked me to have dinner with him on Saturday. Maybe you should consider asking his secretary if she's busy."

* * *

Mary didn't recognize the car which stopped outside her door. She was alone; Susan and Peter had taken the children with their own to a pantomime and they were staying over. She had considered going out but couldn't think of anywhere she wanted to go. Now it was late and she was nervous about the car which stopped so obviously in front of her door. The doorbell rang. Mary, knowing she shouldn't, opened the door. Cal stood there, dressed in a dark suit as though he was going somewhere or had been somewhere.

"Isn't it late for calling?" Mary said, letting him in anyway.

"Yes, it's late."

"I didn't recognize the car."

"It's a hire car. The other will take weeks to fix. Do you have any whisky?"

"No, I haven't. What is this? The last time I saw you you got up and walked out while I was trying to talk to you."

"Did I?"

"Yes, you did."

"I'm sorry. Mary, will you do me a favour?"

Mary wasn't very happy about the

soft tone in his voice.

"What kind of favour?"

"Can I kiss you?"

"What?"

Cal leaned over and put his lips to her neck and when she didn't object he did it again further down and then again further down still and then he reached the buttons on her blouse. Mary stopped him there.

"Whoa. Hey. That's about enough."

"Is it?"

"It is, yes."

Cal looked at her.

"Are you sure you don't have any whisky?"

"Quite sure."

He kissed her on the lips. Very briefly, softly.

"I've been out to dinner with Greta."

"Oh."

"It was the fourth time this week."

"The fourth time?"

"Yes."

"Nice dinner?"

"Very good, yes."

"What did you have?"

"We had smoked salmon and roast duckling and crême caramel. Not like ordinary crême caramel. Out of this world crême caramel."

"I like apple crumble."

"Is that what you had?"

"No, the children are at Susan's. I had a tomato sandwich."

Cal kissed the other side of her neck, all the way down to the same button, only this time he undid the button with deft fingers and then the next one and the fastening underneath. Mary would have loved to have been able to tell him not to. She would have given a great deal to have said the words but she had spent far too many nights wishing that he would do exactly what he was doing so she couldn't. When his hands got as far as the belt on her jeans she found her voice.

"No." That was all. Cal looked at her like somebody who'd been told that crême caramel was off the menu. But he let go of her. Mary moved away, fastened the buttons, pushed her shirt into her jeans.

"The last time we met — "

"Must we have that again?" Cal sounded bored.

"You walked out."

"I had just driven my car into a wall."

"Because I had told you that I didn't trust you."

"That's not why. The road was wet. You don't have to bring it all up again. It has nothing to do with now. It's no good stuffing your shirt into your jeans and pretending you don't want to. If you hadn't wanted to you would have stopped me earlier."

"I did stop you earlier."

Cal said nothing. He just looked at her.

"This isn't how I want things to be," Mary said.

"No?" He looked at her and Mary recognized the look. This was what he was like at work with people who had crossed him, very cool, even-tempered, very much in control. "I thought this was what you wanted. This was how we were to begin with. You didn't want to go any further. You wanted to go to bed because you were too frightened to try for anything more. You're obsessed with the idea of security. You want to bind yourself about with stone walls so that nobody can ever get near."

"That just isn't true. Going to bed with you . . . it isn't like it was — "

"Oh, great. Now I'm no good in bed either."

"It was fun before. I thought when we first met, I thought . . . last Christmas that you were just having a good time. We laughed and joked and you used to kiss me all over my face and it was fun, it was easy. It isn't like that now."

"How can it be like that now?" Cal asked softly.

"You don't talk to me now. You're so cool like I was just any one-night stand, so keen and . . . you used to be gentle and kind and . . . you cared about me. I didn't realize that."

"You didn't want me to care about you."

"I was frightened. My life was nothing but responsibility because my marriage hadn't worked. I used to lie in bed and wish I was a child again. Sundays. Sundays when I was little. My mother used to make roast beef and Yorkshire pudding and my father used to sit by the fire reading the newspaper."

Her childhood had been full of Sundays, snowy days and sledging in the streets, coming home cold to the fire and toast and jam and peaches and cream. There were parties on her birthday, pretty dresses to wear, parcels to unwrap, games to play, friends to laugh with. Long golden endless days. No difficult decisions to be made, a time when the future was possible.

"When somebody cares about you it's better even than that. If Trevor hadn't tried to take the children and we hadn't had to buy Grey House, if things hadn't moved so fast and gone so wrong maybe it would have been better, we would have gradually moved on but it wasn't and all I could think about was how things were when my marriage went bad and how it was after Trevor left. I can't go through that again. I liked having you to myself. I never had anybody to myself before. I wanted for a little while not to be with the children, not for it to be houses and meals and responsibilities but it didn't happen."

Cal said nothing. He didn't even look at her. He was standing near the door. Mary was quite worried that he would make an excuse and leave.

"Are you having dinner with Greta tomorrow?" she asked.

"No."

"Saturday?"

"No, she's going out with Paul."

"Is she?"

He finally turned to her. "This is for the last time of asking," he said. "Will you have dinner with me tomorrow?"

"Yes."

"I'll pick you up at seven," Cal said and then he left.

★ ★ ★

He took her to a very exclusive hotel.

"I thought you were broke," Mary ventured.

"My grandmother used to say 'we may be poor but we mustn't look it.' All I have to do is work like hell for five years to get back to where I was six months ago."

"If this is suffering I can stand it."

"Oh, I see, it's not my body, it's my overdraft that attracts you. Well, don't get carried away. I won't be taking you away from your job and your street house or buying you diamonds for Christmas."

"I already have diamonds," Mary said, moving her head slightly so that the diamond drops in her ears glittered madly. "Though at the time I didn't realize they had cost so very much.

You can have them back for your overdraft."

"No, thanks. I like them best where they are."

They danced until late. Mary's mother had taken the children and to her surprise had seemed pleased to do so. Even when Mary had said where she was going and who with her mother had just nodded and said nothing. Her father hadn't even looked up from the seed catalogue he was reading.

Cal didn't offer to take her home, he took her back to his parents' house.

The house no longer looked like his parents' place. It was Cal's house. There were more books, there was music.

"What is it?"

"It's Bach. Violin concertos. You like it?"

"Yes."

"Have you bought the house from them?" Mary asked, following him into the drawing-room. "I thought you said you had no money."

"My father may be an awkward bastard but he's not that bad. They'll come and stay when they're in the country."

"They've given you the house?"

"Something like that. I take it you approve?"

Mary took a sip of the wine he had handed her and closed her eyes.

"Listen," she said.

"To what?"

"Silence. I live on a street." She waved a generous hand at her surroundings. "Ten acres and your own owls."

"You still bring the children to school here?"

"I didn't want to mess them around. Besides, it's a very good school. It's a good arrangement. I bring them, pick up somebody else's and she collects them and leaves them with Susan until I get back. I don't work as hard for Paul Archer as I did for you. I get back sooner."

"And he pays you more."

"Yes, but he doesn't provide me with

a house like you did."

"I'm sure if you exerted enough effort he would."

"I don't think Paul would be any good with children."

"I knew there was something about me that you liked," Cal said.

"It isn't the only thing about you that I like," Mary said and she put down her wine-glass and she kissed him generously on the mouth.

"I thought you'd decided I wasn't any good at that either."

"Persuade me."

"No way. I've spent a lot of time trying to persuade you into things."

"Please, Cal," and she kissed him again. "I want you to."

"How much?"

"A hundred and fifty per cent."

"Is that all?"

"I've missed you so much. I want to try again. Slowly."

"Slowly? How slowly?"

"Very slowly," and she kissed him again. "I love you, Cal."

Cal fastened his arms tightly around her, closed his eyes, listened to the sound of the owls calling to one another in the garden, and then he kissed her. And he thought back to the day when he had walked into Bob Patten's outer office and first seen her. He was already a cynic by then. Love at first sight was for teenagers. She was wearing cheap clothes but in a colour that suited her and she smiled at him but the smile wasn't a big one, it was for who he was. She had only been there for a few days. After that he had seen her a lot.

"Is she good, Bob?" he asked after a few months.

"The best secretary I ever had. She won't stay."

"Why not?"

"Needs full-time work. She's divorced with two kids and her husband keeps her short. I wouldn't care, but the bastard's got money. Trevor Dickinson, you know, garden centres and the like. Got anybody in mind for Ann's job?"

"Not yet."

"Mind you, you'd have to be careful."

"How d'you mean?"

"She doesn't like men. Not surprising but I mean there's no informality, none at all. Isn't she beautiful? It's a shame. She's a nice kid."

She had come to his office, glancing nervously around. Cal gave her as much charm as he could manage but her eyes didn't change expression.

"My secretary's leaving," he said. "Bob said you need a full-time job."

Mary sat with her hands in her lap and looked straight at him.

"I have two children, Mr Fitzgerald."

"Yes, I know. You can call me Cal if I can call you Mary."

"My children come first with me. That may be a problem."

"I don't see why it should be. Bob says you're the best secretary he ever had. I'll pay you well."

"How much is well?"

Her eyes changed only when he

mentioned the figure.

"That's good money," she said.

"I always pay well for the best."

And then she smiled. Cal hadn't been sure about her before then. After that he didn't know how he was going to get through another day without her.

"I'll think about it," she said. "Can I have a day or two?"

"You can have a week if you like."

When she had gone Cal had stood by the window looking over the yard. It was a warm misty September day. The best month of the year.

*Other titles in the
Linford Romance Library:*

A YOUNG MAN'S FANCY
Nancy Bell

Six people get together for reasons of their own, and the result is one of misunderstanding, suspicion and mounting tension.

THE WISDOM OF LOVE
Janey Blair

Barbie meets Louis and receives flattering proposals, but her reawakened affection for Jonah develops into an overwhelming passion.

MIRAGE IN THE MOONLIGHT
Mandy Brown

En route to an island to be secretary to a multi-millionaire, Heather's stubborn loyalty to her former flatmate plunges her into a grim hazard.

WITH SOMEBODY ELSE
Theresa Charles

Rosamond sets off for Cornwall with Hugo to meet his family, blissfully unaware of the shocks in store for her.

A SUMMER FOR STRANGERS
Claire Hamilton

Because she had lost her job, her flat and she had no money, Tabitha agreed to pose as Adam's future wife although she believed the scheme to be deceitful and cruel.

VILLA OF SINGING WATER
Angela Petron

The disquieting incidents that occurred at the Vatican and the Colosseum did not trouble Jan at first, but then they became increasingly unpleasant and alarming.

DOCTOR NAPIER'S NURSE
Pauline Ash

When cousins Midge and Derry are entered as probationer nurses on the same day but at different hospitals they agree to exchange identities.

A GIRL LIKE JULIE
Louise Ellis

Caroline absolutely adored Hugh Barrington, but then Julie Crane came into their lives. Julie was the kind of girl who attracts men without even trying.

COUNTRY DOCTOR
Paula Lindsay

When Evan Richmond bought a practice in a remote country village he did not realise that a casual encounter would lead to the loss of his heart.

ENCORE
Helga Moray

Craig and Janet realise that their true happiness lies with each other, but it is only under traumatic circumstances that they can be reunited.

NICOLETTE
Ivy Preston

When Grant Alston came back into her life, Nicolette was faced with a dilemma. Should she follow the path of duty or the path of love?

THE GOLDEN PUMA
Margaret Way

Catherine's time was spent looking after her father's Queensland farm. But what life was there without David, who wasn't interested in her?

HOSPITAL BY THE LAKE
Anne Durham

Nurse Marguerite Ingleby was always ready to become personally involved with her patients, to the despair of Brian Field, the Senior Surgical Registrar, who loved her.

VALLEY OF CONFLICT
David Farrell

Isolated in a hostel in the French Alps, Ann Russell sees her fiancé being seduced by a young girl. Then comes the avalanche that imperils their lives.

NURSE'S CHOICE
Peggy Gaddis

A proposal of marriage from the incredibly handsome and wealthy Reagan was enough to upset any girl — and Brooke Martin was no exception.

A DANGEROUS MAN
Anne Goring

Photographer Polly Burton was on safari in Mombasa when she met enigmatic Leon Hammond. But unpredictability was the name of the game where Leon was concerned.

PRECIOUS INHERITANCE
Joan Moules

Karen's new life working for an authoress took her from Sussex to a foreign airstrip and a kidnapping; to a real life adventure as gripping as any in the books she typed.

VISION OF LOVE
Grace Richmond

When Kathy takes over the rundown country kennels she finds Alec Stinton, a local vet, very helpful. But their friendship arouses bitter jealousy and a tragedy seems inevitable.